D1435254

WHEN I SAY YES

NEW YORK TIMES BESTSELLING AUTHOR
LISA RENEE JONES

ISBN-13: 979-8797131649

PART ONE: NEW YORK

CHAPTER ONE

The driver pulls us to a stop next to a sidewalk, and Dash opens the door and gets out. I follow him, but he catches my arm and halts me at the door.

"We don't work. I was selfish to think we worked, Allie. Go home. It's better that way. Neil will watch over you until this Allison thing is figured out. He'll call you. Answer when he does."

My eyes burn and my chest pinches. "Don't do this," I plead. "Don't let him blaming you for something that wasn't your fault divide us."

"How do you know it wasn't my fault, Allie? How do you know anything about me when you don't know that?"

"Don't go and fight, Dash. Brandon and your father, they're watching. This was all planned. They want to take you down. Don't fight. Please. I'm begging you."

"Go home," he says again, and with that bitter command, he releases me, turns, and starts walking. I round the door and intend to follow, and I try, but I make it half a block and he's just gone. I can't see him anymore.

I'm trembling when I climb back into the SUV and shut the door. "Where to, ma'am?"

Where to?

Home, *Dash said. I don't even know where that is right now, but it seems fairly obvious that Dash just broke up with me. I give the driver my apartment address.*

I'm sitting on the bed of my tiny New York apartment, my "home" where I've been sent, tears streaming down my face, as I desperately try to pull myself together. I don't live with Dash anymore. I never really lived with him. I was just staying with him. That much is clear. But as to why this happened, well it's all about my ex, Brandon, and Dash's father, plotting against Dash, trying to hurt him. Trying to set him up.

"Oh God," I whisper as I pull this all together. Brandon taunted Dash about fighting. He has to know about Dash's habit. And what did Dash do? Push me away and clear a path for them to come after him.

"Because he's going to fight," I whisper, standing up and pressing my hands to my face. His fighting started after his brother died. During the confrontation with his father, his father made it clear that he blames Dash for his brother's death. Dash is going to fight. I search anxiously for my phone and find it in my jacket pocket, punching in Dash's number. It goes straight to voicemail and a sound of utter frustration rips from my lips. There's a beep to leave a message and I spill out a plea. "Don't fight, Dash. Brandon and your father are together, two people who want to hurt you. They're watching. They're coming for you. I beg of you, fight the need. Please. I'm here and—"

The machine cuts off. I call back again and it goes to voicemail. I quickly type a message that matches my voicemail and then start to pace. He's going to fight. I know this in my gut as sure as I know my own name. He's going to fight. I halt abruptly and stare at my phone. I can't believe I'm going to do this, but I have no choice. I dial Tyler.

"Ms. Wright. What can I do for you?"

"Allie," I say. "I need to be Allie right now, Tyler, because I need you to act like a friend. To me and to Dash. Because I'm probably about to ruin my relationship with him by coming to you. I know I am."

"Oh fuck," he murmurs. "What the hell is going on?"

"This has to be between you and me, Tyler. Promise me. I need advice. I don't need you to go off the deep end."

"He's fighting," he assumes far too easily for my comfort.

"That's not a promise," I chide.

"I'll protect you, Allie. And him. *Is he* fighting?"

"He's going to," I dare to confess. "I know he's going to. Do you know about the signing?"

"What about it?"

Obviously, he does not know and at the risk of putting Bella on the spot with him I say, "My ex is an agent who is now agenting his father."

"Holy hell. This is clearly going no place good."

"Exactly," I say. "Were talking a cesspool of hate. Dash's father hates him. My ex hates me and so he went after Dash. I should have seen it coming. I should have warned—"

"What did he do?" he demands roughly.

"He turned the signing into a father-son event."

"What? That makes no sense. Dash would never allow that to happen and neither would Bella."

"Brandon got it out to the press, so if either man backed out, they looked bad. They were both cornered to go through with it for the betterment of the charity."

"I assume they both showed up."

It's more a statement of fact but I answer anyway. "Yes."

"What happened?"

"His father cornered us and all but called Dash a killer. He even said something to the effect of Dash eventually killing me, too."

Tyler grunts. "That son of a bitch. Yeah, Dash is going to fight tonight. No question about it."

7

"Where?" I ask. "I need to know where so I can stop him."

"I don't know where and even if I did, you can't go to an underground fight club alone. But I might be able to payoff the right people to freeze him out. Let me make some phone calls."

"Don't tell Bella. Not yet. Not if we don't have to tell her."

"I didn't plan on telling Bella. She'll lose her shit, but Bella should have told me what was going down with this signing. We should have had them sign separately at different times or in different rooms."

He's not wrong, but it all happened so fast, I don't think anyone could even get their head around the best next move. For now, I focus on avoiding another time bomb. "Don't call Dash," I say. "Please. I beg of you. If he knows I went to you—"

"Maybe that would wake his ass up and bring him back to your side."

My heart jackhammers. "Don't. No."

"I got it, I won't call Dash. I'll get back to you soon." He disconnects.

I try Dash again and another call comes through. I quickly switch over. "Hello."

"Allie, this is Neil Ledger."

Neil isn't just some guy. He worked with Dash while they were both in the FBI, and now does private hire work. I'm not sure if he's Dash's friend, but he's sure not his enemy. He wants me to leave New York which means he could be mine.

"Where are you?" Neil asks.

"Home," I say. "Why?"

"I'm sending a car for you. There's a private plane waiting."

Hope fills me as I ask, "Will Dash be there?"

"No," he says solemnly. "No, he's not going to be there."

"Where will he be?"

"He's leaving town."

"Back to Nashville?" I ask, even when I already know that's not going to be Neil's answer.

"No, Allie," Neil says. "Not to Nashville."

Of course not, I think. He wants me in Nashville, and far, far away from him. "Where?"

"I don't know."

"Liar," I accuse, and I don't give him time to lie again with his denial. "I'm not leaving," I say. "I have a job and a home here."

"Dash wants—"

"For me to go home? I am home. And I'm staying here."

"He wants you to go back to Nashville."

And when I'm gone, Dash is going to find the nearest fight club and bury his face in someone's fist and that's essentially what he does. He taunts his opponent into punching him, hurting him, *punishing him*. And he wants me far away when he does it. Because he needs to fight more than he needs me. Dash threw me away with the ease of a boy throwing a ball, and that hurts, it downright guts me, but that doesn't change the fact that I love him. Nor does it wash away my determination to save him from himself. I can't do that by alerting Dash that I'm coming for him. Neil is still on the phone, determined to get me back to Nashville.

"No," I say firmly. "I'm not getting on that plane. I'm not going back. Not now. Maybe never."

I disconnect and I dial Tyler. He answers on the first ring. "I need thirty seconds, Allie. I'll call you back."

Well, at least he called me Allie. If he'd have called me Ms. Wright, I might have screamed at him. "His buddy Neil says he's headed out of town. I think that means he's really staying here. Where will he go if he wants to fight?"

"I told you. I have no idea. I'm working on it now." His phone must beep with another call. "I've got a PI I use on occasion digging around. I need to take this." He disconnects.

I pace again, trying to think what to do. Dash is hungry to fight. He's *going* to fight. I need help and it has to be from someone that won't burn Dash. One name comes to my mind. God, I can't believe I'm going to do this, but I am. I punch the number into my cellphone and listen to the line ring. One time. Two times. Then, "I trust this is important, Ms. Wright."

"Mr. Compton," I say, and then just as I did with Tyler, I add his first name, "*Mark.* This is a personal call. I need help. I *really* need help."

"What kind of help?"

His voice is hard, but then it's always hard. "The kind that could destroy a very high-profile, good man, if I trust the wrong person."

"And you came to me?" I can almost hear his eyebrows lift.

"Yes. You're the most private, well-connected person I know."

"Talk," he orders.

"Do you know who Dash Black is?"

"The author. I do. What about him?"

"I'm dating him. I moved in with him in Nashville, but that doesn't mean I'm not coming back to work. I just—"

"Get to the problem."

"He has a bit of a habit, or addiction, to something that could ruin him. And he—can I just meet you in person? Now?"

WHEN I SAY YES

He's silent a moment. "The coffee shop next to Riptide. Fifteen minutes. Do you need me to send you a car?"

"I'm close. I'll walk. Thank you."

We disconnect and I press my hand to my head. I can't believe I'm doing this, but it's this or nothing and nothing is not an option.

LISA RENEE JONES

CHAPTER TWO

I manage to turn off the faucet on my face and slip out of my coat long enough to fix my makeup. Once that's done, I do what I would never do under normal circumstances before meeting with my boss. I down a glass of wine as if it's a shot of whiskey. I slip back into my coat, grab my purse, and head for the door. But not without turning and looking at my apartment. This is my home. Or maybe my home is another place in Nashville, but it's not with Dash.

My place.

No one can take it from me.

Dash's place was never mine. I know that now.

With the ease that he sent me away, we were never what I thought we were. But to his credit, he warned me. He's not a forever kind of guy. With a twist of my heart, I exit the apartment and lock up. I can't think about what could have been that really never existed as a possibility in the first place. I just have to save Dash from himself, even if it changes my boss's view of me going forward.

The walk is brisk, chilly, the late afternoon cloaked in shadows as the sun begins to hug buildings and fade into the horizon. I can only assume that the fight clubs operate in the dark of night and that night is not far from welcoming him with its false promise of shelter that it doesn't have to offer.

I arrive at the coffee shop and promise myself I will not lose my shit with Mark Compton. I will be calm and confident. I will represent myself and the auction house with dignity. With these vows, I open the door and step inside, a cozy fire in a stone fireplace warming the room. Mark stands and waves at me. He's at a back corner table that allows him a view of the entire coffee shop. It's a position of control and I would expect no less from this man, which is exactly why I believe he can help me.

Hurrying toward him, I sit down, surprised to find a cup of coffee waiting on me. "Vanilla latte," he says as we sit. "Isn't that what you always order when one of the staff picks up coffee for the office?"

"Yes," I say. "How would you know that?"

"I know everything about the people who work for me, Ms. Wright."

"Allie," I say. "Or not. Whatever you want."

He studies me with piercing gray eyes that seem to see right to my soul. He's wearing an olive-green sweater and jeans today, but he's no less intimidating in casual attire than he is in a custom suit. *A lot like Tyler*, I think, only Tyler crossed a line with Dash that somehow took him to another level of personal with me, and that I will never be with Mark Compton. I wonder if anyone is ever that personal with this man.

"Vanilla is a very safe choice, Ms. Wright," he observes, and just when I think that's exactly what he's doing, being personal with me, he adds, "Asking me for help with a personal issue is not. I do believe you're showing a little growth."

I blink. "You think me asking you for help shows growth?"

"You're taking a risk. We both know this is a risk. Talk to me. And to some degree, your role with Riptide will remain stagnant until you learn how to take a risk and do so with confidence. You got the risk right today. You need to work on the confidence."

"Easier said than done when I'm taking that risk with someone else's life. If I tell you this, you could ruin him."

"I have no desire to ruin Dash Black or another man who hasn't done anything to hurt me or those I love. You can trust me, Ms. Wright."

"I believed that before I called you or I wouldn't be here. Your mother knows my story, which means you may or may not, so forgive me for repeating what might not be necessary. My ex is a high-powered entertainment agent. He represented my father as he transitioned from playing football to being a talking head on camera. Leaving out the gory details, I broke up with him and my father did the same."

"I didn't think you spoke to your father?" he asks, confirming he does, in fact, know the story I told his mother before she hired me. Or at least, part of it.

"I don't," I say. "Gossip spills though. An agent told me about it. But as I mentioned, or I think I did—I'm not exactly myself right now—Brandon, my ex, wants revenge. He sees Dash as the way to get it."

"How very predictable," he says dryly. "What did he do to Dash?"

"Dash and his father are not on good terms."

"Didn't I just read about some big signing they did together today?"

"Not by choice. Brandon recruited Dash's father as a client. Then he tricked both men into a signing together. He made a splash with the press so they couldn't back out of the event, which was for a charity. The two of them together went very badly. The confrontation was inevitable, and that connected to a highly personal loss the two share, which drove Dash over the edge. Dash has an addiction, not a conventional one, but an addiction. One he promised me was over."

"That's not how addiction works," Mark points out. "Not a true addiction."

"I know. But he made it seem as if he fell off the wagon, so to speak, but it was under control. I don't believe that now. He pushed me away the minute this fight with his father happened. And of course, I know why."

"He needs his high," he supplies.

"Yes. And this could destroy his career. And he's going to act on this need of his now, tonight, while his father and Brandon are watching. I need to find him before they do."

"What is the addiction?"

"Fighting. Underground fighting. Illegal fighting. There's a place in Nashville I know he's been to, but I don't think he'll leave the city before indulging in that high. He needs it too badly. He has film deals and a TV show in negotiation. If he ends up in the press over this—"

"It won't kill the deal," he assures me. "In fact, it will bring attention to the movies and the books. But that doesn't mean it won't kill him." He picks up his phone from the table. "Lucky for you, I have the right people around me to get you the answers you need." He stands and walks away.

I grab my phone and check for a message from Dash or Tyler, but there is nothing. I text Dash: *Please call me. If you care about me even a little bit, you will call me.*

My cellphone rings and I glance at the caller ID. It's an unknown caller and I know that means Neil. I decline the call and text Dash: *I'm not going back to Nashville, Dash. Not now and maybe not ever. So tell Neil to stop contacting me.*

He doesn't answer. I try to call him. It goes to voicemail. His phone is off. And I know why. He doesn't want to talk to me. He doesn't want to be stopped.

WHEN I SAY YES

My phone buzzes with a text message and my heart leaps with the hope that it's Dash. It's not. It's Tyler: *No luck yet. Still working.*

My lashes lower on a sigh, and a complete utter feeling of defeat. I can't save him. Because he doesn't want to be saved.

LISA RENEE JONES

CHAPTER THREE

Mark leaves me at the table so long that I down my coffee and head to the bathroom, which is large and offers me the privacy to pace. And so, I do. I walk into the one-person bathroom and start pacing. It's a four-step pace and turn, but it helps. After I've done about twenty laps, I wash up, freshen up, and check my phone for the hundredth time. With a deep breath, I exit the bathroom to find Mark and another man waiting on me.

My heart thunders in my chest with the certainty something is wrong. I step to the table and slide uneasily into my chair. The newcomer is blond, with ink down his arms and piercing blue eyes.

"Hi," I say.

"Hi," he says. "You look like I'm your worst nightmare. You don't like ink?"

"Oh God no. I mean, yes. I mean—"

To my shock, Mark laughs. Mark never laughs. I didn't even know he was capable of laughter. "This is Lucifer, Allie. He works for Walker Security."

Walker Security is the company that runs Riptide's security, but their reach is far and wide, worldwide in fact, and their skillset is far beyond what they do for us.

"Lucifer is more than a little comfortable in the underground boxing clubs. Which I know because I bet on a few of his fights. Now you know something dirty that you can hold against us if we burn you."

I perk up. "Do you know Dash?"

"I do know Dash," he says.

My heart sinks. "So, he's been fighting? Often?"

"Not here. Not for a long time. Not since all of his success."

19

Until me, I think, and a part of me wonders if I'm not the problem. If I don't need to just go away. But even if I am the issue, not his father, and this time I do think it's his father, he's neck-deep in trouble now, tonight. I have to pull him out of the quicksand before I can walk away.

"And I'm going to piss him the fuck off if I take you to him," Lucifer adds.

"Oh," I say, my gaze jerking to his. "Oh okay. I just— can you—"

"Take you to him?" he asks. "Sure. I don't care much who I piss off unless they're a client of Walker Security. Your boss just happens to be a client of Walker Security." He leans closer and whispers, "Not that I really care if I piss him off either." He glances at his watch. "It's seven o'clock. The first fight will be at eleven."

"Are you fighting tonight?"

"Not tonight," he says. "I have a job in progress. I keep my play out of my day, if you know what I mean."

"Then you can't do this."

"I'm a client," Mark replies. "I'll pay Walker to do this for you."

My eyes go to Mark's. "You'd do that?"

"Of course, I would. I am."

"Nah," Lucifer says. "I'll do it for free, but there's no way I'm taking you there to the club. It's not the place for a lady. Here's how this plays out. You go home. If Dash is on the card—which I won't know until my inside man calls me back—I'll send a car for you. That car will pull up to the front door. I'll 'bump' into you at the front door and you'll beg for my help finding Dash. Make it loud. Make it obvious."

"And then?" I ask.

"Then I blow you off, but not really. I'll tell Dash some chick is upfront trying to see him. He'll freak, of course, and I'll follow him up front. Just so I can be there if someone causes trouble. You and Dash can then do your thing, whatever that ends up meaning. Cool?"

"Yes," I say. "Yes, thank you, Lucifer." I glance at Mark. "Thank you."

He gives me a barely perceivable nod.

"Will you be there?" I ask.

"Yes, and that's part of the plan. I'll be the way you made it to the club."

"He'll be furious with you," I say. "And if we do work things out, I don't want him to hate my boss. Isn't there another way?" I don't give him time to answer. "Actually, there is. He already hates Tyler Hawk. And Tyler knows about his fighting. Tyler told me where the club is located in Nashville. It would be believable that he tracked down this one as well, though, in truth, he tried and failed."

"No to that," Mark states, his tone absolute. "While Lucifer is inside, someone has to be outside, in case you need help. That means me."

"Jacob can go," Lucifer offers. "I already talked to him. He's on standby. He eyes Mark. "That keeps Mark out of the mix and since Jacob oversees the security team at Riptide," Lucifer adds, glancing at me, "it would be easy to have assumed you'd go to him for help. He'll be the fall guy and no one hates anyone. If everyone agrees, I'll get to work."

"Agreed," Mark states.

"Agreed," I say as well.

"Good," Lucifer says. "Go home, Allie." He slaps his hands down on the table. "More soon."

Mark lifts a finger in my direction, "My car is outside. The driver's been instructed to take you home. He'll also be the one picking you up should Dash show up at the club."

In other words, I'm dismissed but I'm pretty alright with that right about now. I need to think and process on my own before I see Dash tonight. And I will. He'll be at that club. I feel it in my bones. "Thank you both. I know I've said that, but I mean it." I glance at Mark. "I owe you for this."

"Your loyalty is my price, Ms. Wright. And I'm aware that Dash makes that complicated, but I'm a forward-thinking man. I do believe we can find a working solution for all. Go home and drink a glass of wine. You have time to use its influence to calm down, but not fall down."

It almost sounds like a joke, but Mark Compton doesn't tell jokes. Does he?

I decide he does not.

I push to my feet, offer both men small nods, and walk toward the door. A few minutes later, I'm in the hired SUV, and a man I've seen with Jacob a time or two greets me. He's dark, Hispanic, I think, and good-looking, with a friendly disposition. "I'm Adrian. Your guardian angel."

"You work for Walker," I assume.

"Bingo." He pulls us onto the road. "Speaking of bingo. How do you get five sweet, kind, angelic, Christian old ladies at the community center to swear like sailors?"

"Is this a trick question?"

"It's a joke. What's the punchline?"

"Ah, tell them there's no more chocolate?"

He laughs, low and masculine, and says, "No, but that would probably work. The answer is, have a sixth one shout, 'Bingo!'"

I surprise myself and laugh. "Thanks for that."

"Well, hopefully, a ride and a smile are all you need tonight but just in case there's more, put my number in your phone."

I pull out my phone and by the time I'm in front of my building, I've stored his number, Lucifer's, and Jacob's. "Now go try to relax. Hopefully, Dash won't go to the fight night and you won't see me again, unless it's at Riptide."

"Thanks, Adrian," I say sincerely, appreciating all Mark and Walker are doing for me and Dash, even if Dash doesn't appreciate their efforts as I do.

Exiting the vehicle, I huddle into myself and my coat as I run through the night that is far more bitter cold than just the weather, and enter my building. Once I'm at my door, my heart sinks and I realize some part of me hoped Dash would be here waiting. Silly girl. Tricks are for kids. I enter my apartment and glance at my watch. I have hours here to fret before any news will follow. I shiver with the low temperature of my apartment and turn up the heat. With my coat still on, I walk to the kitchen, fill a glass with wine, and read the message I sent to Dash. *I'm not going back to Nashville, Dash. Not now and maybe not ever. So tell Neil to stop contacting me.*

Neil hasn't contacted me again. God, maybe he read the message. Maybe he just wants me to go away and instead I'm riding in with the cavalry to save him. I down the wine and pour another glass. I don't even care just how badly me and more wine mix.

CHAPTER FOUR

Neil does, in fact, call.

After my relief that Dash has not blown me off completely over my message, I check myself. Dash may not have even seen that message. He could be that disconnected, with only one love right now, and it's not me. It's fighting. I don't answer any of Neil's attempts to communicate. There's really no point. I'm not going to the airport. I'm not going anywhere until I hear from Lucifer.

I wait for his call as time ticks by with such excruciating slowness. Trying to stay busy, I change into a casual skirt, boots, and a warm sweater, all of which I'd left here in my closet, in my apartment. Unfortunately, I have no tights left here that are not ripped so my thigh highs are all I have to keep me warm. This brings me to the dilemma of all my personal items that are still in Dash's hotel room, and back in his apartment in Nashville, which was never really mine—I know that now—is a real one. I debate going to the hotel now, when he's gone, when the retrieval of my things would be far less sticky. But then I check myself yet again. I don't know Dash isn't in his room. I know he doesn't want me in his room. After all, he didn't say, "Go to the room, Allie." He said, "Go home." With this painful thought in mind, I inventory my closet and my kitchen, and decide a good way to kill the wait will be a run to the store for basics like coffee, creamer, shampoo, conditioner, and so on.

I do just that and while it keeps me busy, it's a painful dose of reality. I need these things, I think, filling my shopping bag because these things are for my *apartment*, which is my home again.

No.

It was always my home. I was just visiting elsewhere.

I'll fly to Nashville for the critical coordination of the auction, and for Thanksgiving and Christmas, as well. Of course, there is the auction that Dash will be at and I'll have to attend, but I'll stay busy and far away from him.

All of these decisions are made by the time I walk back into my apartment. I unpack my bags with at least an hour left until I will hear something about the fight lineup for the night. I down the last of glass number four of my wine, my mind going back to the cocktail party. To that moment after Brandon had cornered me. When Dash had pulled me into a quiet place, just me and him, the rest of the world shut out. I squeeze my eyes shut and I'm there again.

Dash slides one hand between my shoulder blades and molds me close, and the other holds my head. "Do not be embarrassed with me, Allie. God, woman, I love you so fucking much you don't ever have to be embarrassed."

I blink, stunned, all kinds of crazy emotions flooding my entire body. "You love me?"

He tilts my head back, looks into my eyes, and says, "So fucking much and I don't want you to go back to New York." His mouth closes down on mine in a kiss I feel to my toes, a kiss that is so much more than a kiss. It's passion, it's friendship, it's love.

"I love you, too," I whisper, when his lips part mine. "And I want to stay with you." He strokes my hair from my eyes and says, "Let's get out of here."

"Can you?"

WHEN I SAY YES

"Hell yeah, baby." He closes his hand around mine and leads me to the door.

My phone buzzes with yet another message from Neil, which I ignore. Right now, reality hurls rocks at me. Dash saved me from Brandon. Now it's my turn to save *him* from Brandon. *No matter what the cost to me.* Most likely that cost will be my relationship with Dash, but I'm pretty sure I've already paid that price. And I'm not sure what we had was as real as that moment he confessed his love made it feel to me anyway. Of course, whatever I do won't cost me my job. I owe Mark now, and in a big way for all he's done tonight, but he's apparently a reasonable man under all his arrogance and demand.

My cellphone rings and my heart leaps as I reach for it, anxious for something, anything but my empty apartment and a bottle of wine that I'm drinking alone.

Disappointment jabs at me as the caller ID reads Tyler's number. "Hi," I answer, aware that I owe him an update.

"Tell me you've heard from him."

"No," I say, "but my boss at Riptide is a little more connected to that world than I imagined. He's helping me."

"You told him? Damn it, woman—"

"It's okay," I say quickly. "I trust him. And he gave me a little dirt on himself for reassurance that he won't hurt Dash. I've got this. I've got Dash, too. I'll save him from himself and he'll hate me after. But I'll *save him,* Tyler."

"If he hates you for saving him, you're better off without him. But whatever you do, it needs to be low-profile."

"I know. I've got it handled. I have a plan." And because I know that won't be enough for the man aiding in the management of Dash's career, I spend the next ten minutes sharing details about Walker, Lucifer, and Mark's role in all of this.

"This is a good plan," Tyler assures me. "It's the best possible plan under these circumstances. And the very fact that you just happened to have someone in your path that is also in Dash's path, says there's a bit of fate at hand right now."

"You don't strike me as a man who believes in fate, Tyler."

"There's a lot of things you don't know about me, but there's one thing I want you to know. I'm on his side, Allie. And yours." He disconnects.

I reach for the bottle of wine but my phone buzzes with a text. I abandon the wine to read a message from Lucifer: *I just got word from my inside man. Dash is scheduled to fight tonight. I'm sending Adrian to pick you up.*

CHAPTER FIVE

Adrian is waiting for me outside the SUV, greeting me by opening the back passenger door. I slide inside, stunned to find Mark already present. The minute the door is shut, I whirl on him, and as illogical as my fear is, considering I'm all but ensuring Dash and I are over with our plan tonight, I demand, "What are you doing here? Dash will hate you. I can't do this like this."

"Glad to know you're concerned for your future with Riptide, Ms. Wright, but I've discussed how this goes down with Lucifer in more detail. You and Dash having a blow-up at the front of the club entrance is not a smart idea. That means we need another plan to get you inside. Since I'm a big gambler, it comes with perks. I can get you in through the private fighters' entrance. Dash has his own dressing room. You can talk to him there. Let the blow-up happen *there*."

"Dash will hate you," I reply and turn away from him.

"He doesn't have to know I'm involved. I'll get you in and I'll stay outside. But if he finds out I'm involved and hates me because I helped you get to him, then he's blind and stupid and no better than the ex who created this problem."

I don't know if he's right or wrong. I'm not feeling all that logical right now. Emotions don't breed common sense.

Adrian climbs into the front seat of the SUV and the car begins to move. I sink back against the cushion in acceptance. This is going to happen. There's no way around it. We've been driving all of thirty seconds when I turn and face Mark again. "Stay in the vehicle. I'll tell him I went to the security team from Riptide on my own."

"I can't stay in the car and get you into the facility."

Right, I think. He said that. I know that. "Just please stay as low-profile as possible," I reply. "If he doesn't see you, he'll be too angry to know who got me into the club or to care. At least tonight. I don't know what tomorrow will bring. I can't even think about that right now."

"I'll go back to the vehicle as soon as you go into his dressing room."

"Okay," I say. "Yes. That works." I sink back into my seat and watch the bright New York City lights go by without actually seeing them. *You're doing the right thing, Allie,* I tell myself, and do so on repeat, but my heart races, and my palms grow clammy.

The drive is not short. It's long. It's eternal. It's to an area of the city I've never traveled to, but whatever. I don't care. I just want this to be over. We pull up to a building and halt. Mark glances over at me. "You're doing the right thing. He won't see that tonight. You're intruding on an addiction. The apology, the appreciation, comes later. You need to know that."

He's right. This is going to be painful. "I never thought Mark Compton would be my relationship counselor."

"There's a lot you don't know about me, Ms. Wright," he says, and just when I might compare him to Tyler, he adds what Tyler did not, "and you never will." He reaches for his door. "Stay where you are. I'll come to get you." He exits the car.

I don't stay where I'm at. The last thing I need is for Dash to see me with Mark and think there is something between us. I might be angry with him, I might be hurt, but I'm not mean. Nor do I wish to hurt him the way he's hurt me. I exit the car and huddle into my coat, and not because I'm cold, at least not the kind of cold created by the weather. The kind of cold that chills the heart until it's brittle and broken. Mark rounds the vehicle and both he and Adrian join me at the same moment.

Mark motions us forward and our path leads to a steel door guarded by a tall, bald, bulky, angry-looking man who towers above us all. Mark greets him, shaking his hand. "The little lady is the one I told you about," he says. "She's going to give my money man a talking to before he fights."

In other words, Mark bet on Dash to make this happen for me. God, I owe this man in spades. The doorman smiles at Mark, but still manages to look angry. "I heard you laid some money out on that one tonight. He's here. He just got here about ten minutes ago." He motions me to the door. "Last door on the right at the end of the hallway. Talk to our boy, sweetie, but don't fuck him. Fucking a man before a fight fucks him up. We want our big gamer here happy."

I suck in a breath at the brazen words as Adrian opens the door and motions me forward. "You got this," he says softly. "And if you don't, Lucifer will be inside waiting on you, and I'll be here keeping the door company."

His words zap just enough of the adrenaline I'm feeling to steady my knees. I've brought the cavalry and while that might make me feel better, somehow, I don't think it will do the same to Dash. I nod and enter the hallway and I swear my heart is racing all over again. What am I doing? Dash sent me away. He doesn't want me here. He made his choice and it wasn't me. It *wasn't* me.

I'm almost to the end of the hallway and I halt. *He made his choice.*

I'm about to turn, but have second thoughts. I came here because I want to save him, I remind myself, not because he wants me to do this. I came despite the fact he does not want saving. I've run a lot in my life. I will not run now.

Decision made, resolve firmly I place, I march forward and step into a room lined with lockers with a few half-naked men milling about. Lord help me. One of them turns and looks me up and down. I cut right to the first door and I don't knock. I just walk in. And to both my relief—yes, I've found him—and unnerving—my God, he really plans to fight, I find Dash.

CHAPTER SIX

Just seeing Dash and my emotions are a jumbled mess. I feel everything for this man when I'm with him. It's silly, I know. It's too much and too *everything*.

Maybe I should define it as too much.

That's what tonight has proven.

I feel too much for Dash Black.

He's in sweats, naked from the waist up, wrapping his wrist. His body is perfect, as hard as his expression when he looks up and finds me standing there.

The instant he registers I'm the one in his room, his arms drop to his sides, his jaw flexing. "What the hell are you doing here, Allie?" His voice is low, taut like his mood.

"I came for you," I whisper, then in a stronger voice, I say, "I came to save you from yourself."

"You don't belong here."

"No," I agree readily, "but neither do you."

I blink and he's in front of me, caging me to the door without ever touching me, a hand on either side of my head. I want him to touch me. God, how I want him to touch me. "Dash—"

"The person you know is not who I am when I'm here," he growls. "Do you understand? That is not who I am here."

I don't know what that means, but I don't like the pinch in my chest those words create. "You said you wouldn't do this again."

"I said a lot of things we both wanted to believe. They were all *bullshit*."

"Say what you want, Dash. Hurt me. Grind my heart into pieces. It's fine. I knew what I was getting into with you, but if you do this, if you fight tonight, Brandon and your father will find out. And they win. They get what they want. They will hurt you."

"Do you think I give a shit?"

I want to touch him but something holds me back, something tells me he won't react well. "I know you want to punish yourself," I say instead. "I know you blame yourself for your brother's death, even if in your core, you know it's not your fault."

"You know nothing about my brother."

"But I know *you*. And I've seen how shitty your father can be. Punish yourself if you must, but don't do it to their benefit. Keep it private. Go to another damn country and fight, Dash. Don't do it here. Don't do it now."

"Go *home*, Allie."

"I'm already home, Dash. We both know it. No matter what decision you make, I'm done. I'm not going back to Nashville. Not to live. Not even to work." Someone knocks on the door and then it opens, shoving me into Dash as it does.

He catches me to him, the touch electric, powerful, and whatever was ever between us is here now. His eyes meet mine and a punch of awareness blasts into us. But Dash doesn't react by holding me tighter. He sets me firmly away from him and his gaze lifts toward the door. I turn to find yet another big, burly man in the entryway. He eyes me and then Dash. "Mario wants to see you."

I'm still reeling from the way he set me away from him with such decisiveness, with a decision in the action. A decision that said he chose fighting, not me, not even himself because fighting could end badly in all kinds of ways—hurt him, hurt his career. I turn to face Dash but I don't meet his stare. "I'll let you get back to what's really important to you." I rotate and duck under the giant man's arm and all but run toward the door while my eyes blur with tears and the room spins. I can't get out of here quickly enough and once I'm at the door, I shove it open and keep walking.

Adrian is instantly by my side. "Allie, what happened?"

"I just need out of here," I say. "Please take me home."

All of a sudden, someone catches my arm and I'm spun around to face Dash. "What the hell are you doing, Allie?" he demands.

"Go inside, Dash. The press will find you out here." I try to jerk away.

He pulls me closer and his gaze lifts to Adrian. "Who the fuck are you?"

"He's with Walker Security," I say. "The security team for Riptide. They found you as a favor. Obviously, I should have saved the favor for a better time."

His gaze jerks back to mine and he catches my hand. "Come with me." He starts walking quickly. I can barely keep up. My heart is racing. My entire body is quaking.

"Dash, stop!" I call, all but falling down.

He doesn't stop. A man I don't know appears beside yet another SUV and opens the rear passenger door. Dash halts us right there. "Joseph, my driver, will drive you. Go home."

My heart sinks with the realization that he's going back into the fight club, he's going to fight. And yes, I could argue with him, but I don't even know what the point is right now. The sooner I'm inside the vehicle, the sooner I'm away from him. And that's what we both want. Away. From each other. Being with him hurts too much. Being with him tells me what a fool I was and am.

"Yes," I say. "I do believe it's time for me to go home."

I slide inside the vehicle. Dash leans in and looks at me, his eyes burning into mine, but he says nothing. He eases back outside and shuts the door. My brittle, cold heart shatters into a million pieces. My cellphone rings with Mark's number. I answer. "Hi." My voice is weak, but then, my heart is broken. How can it not be?

"What are you doing?" he demands softly.

"Not what he thinks. I'm not leaving. I'll be at work Monday morning."

"You sure about that?"

"Yes. Very."

"If you need help—"

"You already helped. You gave me the chance to see things bright and clear."

"Ms. Wright—"

"Allie," I say, thinking I'm nobody to anyone right now, not even my boss. "I'm Allie." I disconnect.

Joseph is behind the wheel and we're already moving. I decide to be strategic with Joseph. He's not going to drop me at my apartment when that's not what Dash ordered him to do. He's going to take me to the airport. "I need to go to the hotel to pack."

He eyes me in the mirror. "Understood."

I sink back against the seat and start replaying the exchange with Dash. He was cold. Brutally cold. As if there had never been any warmth in him for me at all. I text Tyler: *I found him. But he's going to fight. I can't change that. And don't call. I'll call you tomorrow. I can't talk now. I just can't. I'll call you tomorrow.*

I hit send and slide my phone into my purse.

Twenty minutes later, we arrive at the hotel and luckily Joseph promises to wait out front, as he can't leave the SUV unattended. I hurry inside the building, racing through the lobby, a plan in place. Once I'm in our room, I quickly pack my clothes, *my* clothes. I leave everything Dash bought me. I wasn't with him for gifts and fancy travel. I was with him for him, though I'm not sure I even know who that is anymore.

As soon as I have everything I need, I walk to the door, but I can't say I don't look back.

I do.

And I do so with tears in my eyes.

Instead of exiting the front door where Joseph will be waiting, I leave via a side exit. Now on the sidewalk, headed away from the hotel, I lug the heavy bag down the sidewalk, struggling with every bump and jolt, as if this night can't get any suckier. Tears stain my cheeks when I finally walk into my apartment and drop the bag, sinking to the floor, my body quaking. I need to be alone. I can't be with a man. I choose all wrong. I chose so wrong. And this time, *this time*, I really fell in love.

I eye the bottle of wine and force myself to my feet. I'm going to get drunk. I never get drunk, but I want to right now. I have to numb this pain. I leave my things at the door and march behind the small island—which seemed so impressive in my little apartment when I rented it, but not so much now—and fill a glass. I down several long swallows.

I have to call my mom tomorrow and tell her what's going on. No. I have to figure out what I'm doing and I can't do that yet. Not in this state of mind. I down the rest of the wine and refill my glass. This time I walk to my bedroom and pull back the curtains to stare at my view. A building is my view. Why did none of this feel crappy before now?

I could blame Dash, but it's more about Nashville. I missed it. I chased a dream to New York, achieved the dream, but the dream wasn't everything I'd hoped. I like Hawk Legal. I think I can make a difference there. And if Mark is willing, maybe I can pull my two worlds together and create one perfect one. With my mother close. With Dash close, but without him in my life.

I can't make decisions based on a man.

Never again.

Never again.

Suddenly there's a knock on the door, a pounding that jolts me to the point I almost spill my wine.

"Allie! Open up. I know you're in there."

At the sound of Dash's voice, I tremble inside.

He's here. He's not at the fight club. He's not fighting there, but as he pounds on the door and calls out my name again, "Allie!" it's clear he is *here* to fight. Fine. Bring it. I'm ready for a fight.

CHAPTER SEVEN

I set my glass down, liquid splashing over the sides, the buzz of wine all too present—a mistake no doubt, but this night is filled with mistakes. Why not add yet another fight with Dash to the list? By the time I'm at the door, he's calling out, "Allie, damn it! Open up."

"I have neighbors, Dash!" I grab the door and swing it open, give his unharmed face a quick inspection, and demand, "Don't you have a fight to be at?"

He steps forward, crowding me. His hands are on my waist and he's walking me backward into the apartment and slamming the door shut. "What the hell, Allie?" he demands.

"You're cursing at me again, Dash," I snap. "Damn you."

"Hell yes, I am. I told you to go home. Neil was supposed to tell you to he was sending a driver to take you to the airport." He looks around at the tiny space and says, "*This* is not your home. We have a home in Nashville."

"Because what I earned on my own isn't good enough for your taste?" I snap.

"Because anywhere that's not with me is not good enough."

"Anywhere you can order me to is not a home. It's a prison. I'm not a possession, Dash. And don't treat me like I'm a member of a harem who does as you command." I twist away from him, putting space between us and holding up my hands. "No more. I went into this—whatever this was—with you, knowing I would get hurt. Now, it's happened. Now, I can't do this anymore, Dash. No more."

39

"There's no harem, Allie. There's just you."

"Seems more like there's just *you*. Go fight. Do what makes life livable for you."

"I'm here right now for a reason. You're what makes life livable. *You.*"

"Liar," I accuse. "I'm done with the lie that was us, Dash. I'm done. Go box. Go do you."

I blink and he's closed the space between us again, his hand cupping my head, and dragging my mouth to his. "I don't want you to be done. I'm not done."

"You told me we weren't good for each other anymore."

"I told you I wasn't good for you."

"And then you told me to go home. And that's what I did."

"If this is home, then we'll live here."

His breath is warm. His body is hard and even warmer. "Stop," I hiss, shoving on his chest. "You chose, Dash. And it wasn't me or us."

To my shock and with a stab to my heart, he releases me then, almost as if I've reminded him of a truth, a reality that still exists. He turns away, giving me his back, dragging a hand through his hair. It's then that I realize he's not even wearing a coat. He's in a white T-shirt and jeans, muscles bunched up in his shoulders. He faces me. "I was trying to save you, Allie. From me."

I laugh without humor. "I told you before. It's too late for that. I'm pretty sure it was too late the day we met."

"No," he says. "No, it's not too late. But it will be if I don't leave now." He rotates away from me again and then he's at the door, his hand on the knob.

My heart thunders in my chest and the room spins. If he walks out of this apartment, we're *done*. We're *over*. And he's going to. I *know* he's going to leave. A part of me wants to scream at him to come back. The other part of me wants him to just go, just get it over with so I can try to move on. *Yes, leave, Dash,* I think, but that's not what my heart really wants and the words that follow are ripped straight from my soul. "I used to think I was the one who ran. But I was wrong. All you do is run and hide, Dash." His hand is still on the doorknob, but it doesn't turn and he doesn't move. He is more stone than man right now, impenetrable, and I can't hold back.

I'm unleashed now, my tongue loosened from the wine. "That's what fighting is to you. A way to hide in the punishment, wallow in the pain, and never do the work to get beyond it. I'm part of that work. Being with me makes you have to look me in the eye and that's worse than in the mirror, apparently."

Seconds tick by and then he moves and not to open the door. I blink and he's in front of me, his fingers diving into my hair once more. "Holy hell, woman," he murmurs, and then his mouth is crashing down on mine, and he doesn't give me time to object. He owns me with his mouth, claims me with the licks of his tongue and the taste of man, whiskey, and demand.

I moan with the feel of his hand sliding up my back, molding me closer. "If you want to know everything, Allie," he says, pressing his lips to my neck and then my ear, "you have to give everything."

Guilt stabs at me with the knowledge that I have yet to tell him everything, but then, he never gave me the chance. "Stay long enough for me to get the chance and I will."

His hand slides over my head, over my hair, and tilts my face to his. "And what if you can't?"

"What if I can?" I challenge.

"Yes," he says softly, his voice raw, vibrating. "What if you can?"

It's a question. It's a challenge. It's a promise of happiness tainted with the possibility of failure. It's a twisty road with steep drops and a crash that could rip the very life from our light grip. Or perhaps we're inside a mighty dark forest of trauma and history, of pain and torment, and we're there without a weapon or any protection. Monsters lurk in this forest—our monsters, and they are evil, fanged beasts. One looks like his father. One looks like mine.

His hand slides from under my hair and cups my neck, and he drags my mouth to his. "Now would be the time for *you* to run, Allie."

There's a shift in his energy, a stark punch of hunger and demand beneath his surface. His free hand slides up to the front of my sweater, and he yanks the front, hard and fast, and all the way down. I gasp as the little buttons that held it together pop and fly everywhere.

"I liked this sweater," I whisper, even as he drags it down my shoulders, but he can't be bothered with removing it. His hands are already shoving down my bra, his gaze devouring my breasts, fingers teasing my nipples.

His hot, lusty stare meets mine as he says, "I'll buy you ten just like it for the view."

There's something more than heat in his eyes, something that tells a story. I recognize then what I saw in him when he fought in Nashville. He takes a beating during his fights, but in the end, he conquers, he wins. Tonight, he didn't fight. He didn't conquer. Now, he wants that high, craves it, and I'm where he'll find that relief.

He wants to conquer me.

He wants, needs, and even demands my submission. Because submission is trust and tonight tried to tear away the new and fragile trust between us. A couple of revelations come to me then with surprise. Dash can ask for anything and I'd say yes, which makes him dangerous, so very dangerous. I *should* run, but even after all that happened in the just passed, roughly managed hours behind us, I have less desire to do so than ever.

I love him. I lust for him. I desire him in every possible meaning of that word. I want Dash Black in a bad way. He tears his shirt over his head, tosses it aside, rippling muscles inviting my hands, but even as I reach for him, he catches my arms, presses them behind me, and captures my wrists with his hand. He pulls me firmly against his hard body and I gasp with the feel of him, so dominant, so strong, so intimately close.

"I came here instead of fighting, but all the feelings that took me to the fight club are still right here in me. What are you doing to do about it?"

"What do you want to do about it?"

"Let me fuck you hard and dirty," he says, "all night long. And then, I want to get up and do it again."

"Am I supposed to object?"

"I sure as hell hope not, but maybe you should ask what hard and dirty means."

I've always known there was a darker, edgier part of Dash that he's never unleashed on me, he's never really shown me. It's the part of him that lives in that fighting ring. It's the part of him that is too tormented to ever be gentle. It's the part of him that has been hidden that I want exposed, that I want to know. My fingers catch his belt loops. "Or maybe you should just show me."

LISA RENEE JONES

CHAPTER EIGHT

Dash leans in and presses his cheek to my cheek, his lips to my ear, his breath a warm seductive tease on my neck, I feel in every part of me. "Be careful what you ask for, baby," he says softly.

My fingers curl on his chest. "I won't regret anything with you, Dash." I ease back to look at him. "One day you'll know that."

"Or you'll know," he says, a hidden meaning behind those darkly cloaked words, but there's no time for questions.

His mouth crashes into mine, in a kiss that is all about possession, but there is also torment and pain. He is broken and he doesn't seem to understand that I'm just as broken. Nor does he seem to understand that somehow, some way, when I'm with him, I'm whole again.

Dash's hands slide into my skirt that is unzipped at this point, and he presses it over my hips and down my legs. The moment it's at my ankles and I am in nothing but a tiny piece of lace and thigh highs beneath boots— which truly is kind of a ridiculous combination—but Dash doesn't seem to notice or care.

He lifts me to the island, watching me with an intense look as he unzips my boots, his fingers a tease on my ultra-sensitized skin as he tosses one and then the other away. His need for control is displayed in every part of his life, in the quality of his books, in how he approaches everything, most definitely in how he cares for his body. He is sculpted, masculine perfection, a product of hard work. A work of art.

His hands come down on my legs. "I want you, Allie," he murmurs, his thumb stroking the inside of my leg, heat radiating from that spot all the way up to my sex. "Like I have never wanted anyone in my life."

There is a raw, tormented quality to his voice, almost as if he doesn't want to feel what he feels right now for me. But I know this isn't about me, it's about him. It's about how much he hates himself. How deep that hate runs. There are shadows in the depths of those blue eyes of his that tell his story, a story he allows only me to see.

"Open for me," he orders, a gentle nudge to my knees, but he doesn't do more.

He is asking me to give myself to him, taking but not demanding, and right now, in his current state of emotional upheaval, this means everything. The look on his face is all heat and lust, the warmth of his touch on my body promising me that this night has only begun, and a deep ache radiates in my sex. I do as he bids, as he's *requested*, and I open my legs. Satisfaction slides over his handsome face and his gaze sweeps over my breasts, and my breasts are heavy, my sex tight, wet, aching for him.

Dash catches my fingers and steps between my legs, leaning into me as he presses my hands behind me on the counter. "Hold them there," he says, his mouth right above mine. "Understand?"

Like I have a choice, I think, considering the angle of my body, but what I say is, "And if I don't?"

"My tongue will stop whatever it's doing at the time," he promises, that dark quality I've glimpsed in him oh so present right now, right here.

"That's cruel," I accuse.

His eyes narrow, his jaw clenches. "Now you're starting to understand me."

There's so much self-hate in that statement, that I whisper, "Dash, damn it, stop."

"You're cursing at me, Allie," he says as one of his hands covers my breast, his fingers teasing my nipple, sending a rush of heat through my body.

"Yes," I manage in a raspy voice. "Yes, I am. And you know why."

His teeth nip my lip, and I yelp with the sting, but already he's licking the offended skin, soothing it. A kiss follows, a deep slide of his tongue that burns through me for reasons that reach beyond the heat of this moment. He is here with me, but he is never all here. Not even now.

It doesn't matter though, I'm moaning again, my body heavy, drugged with sensations. "Don't move, cupcake," he murmurs, kissing my chin and then my neck, before his mouth is on my nipples, sucking, licking, *teasing*.

I want to touch him. I can't touch him. Not at the angle I'm leaning and with the pressure of both our bodies forcing my hands to stay the bridge between us and the counter. Dash moves lower, sliding between my legs where he licks my clit. I suck in a breath, my entire body lit up with that one little intimate contact that doesn't last. He moves to my knee, kissing a path up my leg, and when I think I can't take it another moment, he rewards me with another lick of my clit. Then his mouth is gone again, leaving me panting as he finds the other knee. I'm losing my mind as he repeats the same process, kissing a path up my leg, and he offers me another lick. Sensations rock me, but I steel myself for the tease to follow yet again, but it doesn't come. Dash suckles me and my head falls backward, my lashes fluttering with the pleasure, but some part of me screams that this isn't what I expected. This isn't him fucking me hard and dirty all night long. This is *not* the way he lives in the moment, this is not how he uses me to stay here, not underground fighting.

This is not how he fights one obsession with another. This is not how he uses physicality to fight off his demons. This is him pushing that all aside, pretending it doesn't exist.

My body objects—oh how it objects—but I sit up and Dash lifts his head and looks at me. "Allie?"

My answer is to wrap my arms around his neck, my naked breasts between us, heat and desire tamed only by the questions in his eyes and the challenge in my own. "What happened to fucking me hard and dirty and getting that fight out of your system?"

"I assure you, cupcake, me between your legs is better than any fight."

"Bullshit. You went there. You sent me away. You need more than this."

His hands slide around me, between my shoulder blades, his voice roughened as he says, "No. No, I don't need more than this. Not now. Not ever."

"Bullshit," I say again. "Fuck me the way you need to fuck me to never do what you did tonight to me—no, to *us*—again."

"I don't know what you're talking about, Allie."

I catch his hair and not gently. "Bullshit times three and I don't know if I've ever said that word in my life. I don't even like it. Don't make me say it again." I nip his lip and not gently. "Use me."

"Allie," he whispers, his fingers flexing on my back. "Baby, I am."

"If that were the case, your hand would be on my throat and I'd be shoved against the island with a palm on my ass."

"You brought me down." His voice quakes, barely noticeable, but it quakes.

"Liar," I hiss. "All you do is hide from me, Dash. You can't do that anymore. We can't do that. *I* can't do that. I won't do us that way. If you can't be you with me, if you can't use me for an escape, we can't be together. I want everything. Do you understand? All or nothing, Dash. All or nothing."

I'm breathing hard. My heart is racing. And yet, he doesn't move. He just holds me there, breathes with me, seconds, heavy seconds, ticking by, until suddenly his hand is in *my hair*, and he's dragging my head back with an erotic tug, his mouth over my mouth. "You want everything?"

"Yes," I rasp out. "If you dare, but I don't think you do."

"You want my hand on your ass?"

No man has ever had his hand on my backside but Dash. No man has ever been rough and erotic and full of demand but still so damn careful, so tender. Except for Dash. I'm a mix of emotions that rush through me in a rainbow of colors. I don't understand why I need what I need with Dash, how he brings that person to the surface, but it's me, it's the me I never knew and need to know. And it's him. It's all that I can be with him. "Yes," I dare. "Yes. I do."

He kisses me, a wild, hungry kiss, and in the midst of the passion, he scoops me up, cupping my backside and carrying me toward the only other room in the apartment. The bedroom.

LISA RENEE JONES

CHAPTER NINE

Dash carries me to the bedroom and lowers me to my feet at the end of the mattress. I reach for him, and I can feel his need to feel my hands on his body, but instead of caving to that burn, he catches my wrists again. "Not until I say you can touch me."

Defiance rips through my body and my chin tilts. "And if I touch you anyway?"

"Then you won't feel my hand on your ass, baby. Or anywhere else." He drags me closer, aligning our bodies. "You know what I want. *Tell me*. What do I want, Allie?"

"Control," I say without hesitation, but there's a hint of vulnerability in my voice that I cannot tame. Just as I know I will never tame Dash. And the thing is—I don't want to. In fact, I want the opposite. I want him unleashed. I want him wild and free.

"Are you going to give it to me?" he presses. "Can you trust me that much, Allie?"

Trust.

That's the monster that torments each of us in our own minds and yet, we want it from each other, we demand it be given blindly, irrationally perhaps, but it doesn't seem to matter. So much about how Dash and I approach each other is irrational and yet somehow, we make sense. And so I say, "I already do."

He turns me to face the bed, one hand cupping the side of my neck under my hair, the other on my waist, his hard body at my back. Dash leans in close and says, "I can be demanding, Allie."

My mind flashes to the night of our fight back in Nashville, when my hands had been pressed to the front door of our apartment, his hand on my throat, him behind me, thrusting into me. "I know," I whisper, my skin flushing with the memory and because it's the truth, now I dare add, "I like it."

"Do you?" he challenges.

"Beyond reason," I whisper.

His fingers flex on my neck, seconds ticking by before he replies with, "I used to think I wanted to scare you off, Allie."

"And now?"

"Now, I pray I can't." His teeth scrape my shoulder, rasping roughly.

I suck in a breath at the rough, erotic nip that borders on a bite. He cups my jaw and drags my head back to his shoulder, just enough to angle my mouth to his and lower his to mine. "But that doesn't mean I won't try," he adds. "Nice guys are gentle, Allie. You need to know that I'm not a nice guy."

"If I'd wanted nice, I would have walked away before we ever started calling me cupcake which was almost the moment I met you, Dash."

It's a joke about the nickname I've earned with him, but he doesn't laugh or smile. He brushes his lips over my lips. "You taste like you don't know what you're asking for."

"And you taste like you talk too much, Dash Black."

He lingers there a moment, his breath rushing over my lips with a promise of a kiss that doesn't come. Instead, he says, "No more talking. Knees on the mattress, baby."

CHAPTER TEN

This isn't just a moment of vulnerability with Dash. On some level, it's *the* moment.

There's a past in this room though, one that Dash doesn't understand. A past that has my mind singing with insecurity while my heart tells me to lean into an opportunity to move to a new level of intimacy with Dash, to overcome the barriers between us. And there are barriers, all of which we pretended didn't exist when I moved in with him.

But we both knew they did.

My body ignores my mind and my history that I've all but buried because of Dash. My body screams with the need to simply touch him. And Dash's touch is always just what I need, never too far, and somehow farther than I ever expected I wanted or needed. I inhale deeply, and just do it. My knees hit the mattress, but I don't go down doggy style, despite the fact that I think this is what Dash wants from me. I'm just not that bold. Instead, I walk a few inches forward and ease back on my haunches, my hands on my knees. There's silence behind me, complete silence, and goosebumps lift on my skin, anticipation driving me wild.

The past was never about anticipation.

The past was about other things. Bad things that I pretended were good.

This is not the same.

I've seen Dash wild, fucking me hard and fast, and to the extreme. That was good. It gave me the chance to get lost, not to think too much. It forced me to see who he was and what he needed, and somehow, it was never too far.

That isn't now, this isn't what I expected. This is a slow burn. It's a game. We're playing a game, a slow, excruciating game. Because it's not about anger and hurt and everything his father said to him now. He's past that, at least for now. This is about the aftermath, about how it affected us. And this allows me to think almost too much.

This is a test. Dash wants to know how much his father's words affected me and us. And I need to know what he will do when he has my willing control. Will he go too far? Can this man ever go too far with me?

The idea of too far starts to punch at me with memories that I shove aside.

When I believe I can take the silence no more, *finally*, there's the sound of clothing rustling, of Dash undressing, and I'm aware that I'm not supposed to turn, but I want to turn. I want so many things right now. All of them behind me and somehow in front of me. Oh, the irony of what was and is and could be. Seconds tick by, and I find myself hyper-focused on just that—what could be. What will be, now, with me naked on this bed? I don't have to wait long for that answer.

The mattress shifts and Dash is beside me, his hand on my back, between my shoulder blades, but he touches me nowhere else.

I don't know why I'm shy right now, why I resist looking to my left where I will find him, but I do. *That's a lie*, I think. I know why. I'm afraid of what he might see in me. That is until his fingers tease my nipple, and my sex clenches with the intensity of my body's reaction. I catch his hand and look at him, aware of his naked body, of his thick, heavily veined erection between us, but it's his eyes that capture me. "Dash," I whisper, not even sure why.

"I told you, baby. You touch when I tell you to touch."

"Now," I say softly, emotions welling inside me, the intensity of what I feel for Dash hard to even explain. "I want to touch you now."

"And I want you to, cupcake. Just not yet. Lean forward and press your hands to the mattress."

I draw in a breath as I realize he does indeed want me on my hands and knees. I can't do it. Not right now. I'm so afraid of what that will make him feel, but I just act. I rotate into him, press my body to his. "I need to tell you something."

Dash folds me close and cups my head. "You already told me."

"No," I say, panting out a breath. "No, don't say I don't trust you. That's not what this is."

"I wasn't going to say that at all. I don't need you to go too far, too fast, baby. That's not what I need at all. And I don't need that fight club. I just need *you*."

My heart squeezes. "You do?"

"I do," he says again, "and I know what you need, what we need."

He moves to the headboard and pulls me to his lap, me straddling him, the thickness of his erection pressed to my backside, while his hand is on my face. "This," he says, and then he's kissing me, and I can taste tenderness on his lips and so much more. There is honesty and passion. There is love and need and hunger.

My hands are on his shoulders, my naked breasts between us, his hands cupping them, thumbs stroking my nipples. I lean into his palms and press my mouth to his mouth. He cups my head and then he's kissing me again, and this kiss is different. This kiss is demanding, greedy, and intense. That wildness I'd expected from him is back again and it seduces me, claims me.

I'm kissing him with all that I am, touching him with hungry hands, muscles flexing beneath my fingers. And he is touching me, his hands all over me. It's just not enough. Nothing is ever enough with Dash. There's nothing but him and me, and me and him, right now.

"Dash," I pant out. "Dash."

"I know, baby. I know." He catches my waist and lifts my body, adjusting, his shaft now between us.

I reach down and touch it, and he groans, that rough, masculine sound urging me forward.

I guide his cock between my legs, press him inside me. He's so big, so thick and hard, I moan as he fills me, and I can barely catch my breath. I pant as I slide down the length of him, take all of him until we're skin to skin, consumed by one another.

Our eyes meet and we just stay there, locked together, unmoving.

There's this connection between us that I don't know how to explain, it's both sexual and emotional, magnetic, addictive. The air thickens and seems to burn with that connection and Dash tangles his fingers in my hair and drags my mouth to his. "He hurt you."

"What?" I gasp, shocked at his observation.

"I saw it in your eyes, baby. He hurt you. I will *never* hurt you."

I drop my chin and my lashes lower with the impact of those words on our relationship. I try to push away from him, but he folds his arm around me. "Don't run, baby. Don't run."

"I'm not glass that will break, Dash. One minute you want to fuck me hard and dirty and now you think I'm too weak or you think—"

"No. I don't. You are the strongest person I've ever known, Allie Wright. You make me stronger."

"And yet you want hard and dirty, and you give me gentle and sweet.

"And what if you don't?"

"Stop protecting me from you, Dash. That doesn't work for us. Stop."

He doesn't reply. He doesn't speak but we're breathing together, and a spark seems to ignite all over again. Dash drags my mouth to his and he's kissing me, wildly, hotly, and any reserve I'd had evaporates. He's cupping my head, my breast, rocking with me, his cock pressing into me. And I'm riding him, rocking with him, swaying against his body.

We're *fucking*.

And yet, it's so much more.

He consumes me and I consume him. There is no time, no past—there isn't even a future. There is just right here, right now, or so I think. Dash squeezes my backside and says, "You won't break," before he smacks my ass.

I gasp and he thrusts into me, a sweet burn where his hand and cock torment me. I bury my face in his neck, and he does it again. I can feel my fingernails digging into his shoulder. "More?" he asks me, his hand on my face, dragging my gaze to his. "More, Allie?"

"God, yes," I plead, and that's what he gives me. More. And more. Of his hand, his mouth, his body pressed inside my body. And it doesn't take much before I am at the place of no return. I go from holding back, trying to make this last, trying to hold onto every last second of this, *all of this,* to tumbling over that edge none of us ever want to fall from just yet, to that place of ultimate bliss. My body jerks, and the spasms of my sex around his cock follow. His arm is back around my waist, and he drags me down against him, thrusting with a lift of his hips, a rough, guttural sound rumbling from his chest and lips. I shudder. He quakes. We eventually collapse into each other.

I'm draped forward, over his shoulder, when time comes back to me. Dash grabs a tissue from the bedside. We end up on our backs, naked and staring up at the ceiling. The implications of all that just happened, of what I somehow confessed without confessing, come back to me. "How did you know?" I ask softly, turning my head to look at him.

I find that he's already looking at me. "I saw it in your eyes. What did he do to you, Allie?"

My gaze returns to the ceiling and I decide that I was wrong. I wasn't vulnerable when I leaned over the bed, naked. That wasn't the test. This is the test, my willingness to bear my soul.

CHAPTER ELEVEN

What did he do to you?

Dash's question hangs in the air, deserving of an answer.

Fighting for words—no, fighting my embarrassment—I sit up and scoot to the edge of the mattress. Dash grabs the blanket at the end of the bed and pulls it around my shoulders, as if he understands that naked is *really* naked right now. He stands and grabs his pants, pulling them on, leaving them low-slung and unzipped as we both sit on the side of the bed.

When I still haven't spoken, Dash glances over at me. "Do you know why I fight?"

"Tell me," I urge, eager for this look into Dash's mind, eager for an escape from my own.

"I give the other guy control. Then, I take it back. I make sure he knows I always had control."

"What are you saying?"

He strokes the hair from my face and tilts my face to his. "You always have control with me, baby. You say no. You say yes. Remember that."

"If that were true, you wouldn't have gone to fight tonight."

"Did I fight?"

"No. No, you didn't fight. Well, except with me."

"And I didn't win, nor did I want to win. Submission isn't weakness, Allie," he says, and suddenly I don't believe we're talking about his fight tonight. "It's a choice. What we just did, that was about—"

"Trust," I supply. "I do trust you, Dash."

"I didn't do much to deserve it tonight."

"Yes, you did. You walked away from the fight."

"Well, that was my point I was getting to. That was me submitting to you."

I laugh. "You did not submit. You never submit."

His lips curve. "No?"

"No," I say, but my mood shifts back to serious. "And I don't want you to, either." I twist around to face him. "Don't stop fighting for me. Stop for you. It's destructive. I know you know that."

His jaw sets hard and he closes his hand over mine, a sign he is present and with me, but his gaze shifts forward. "It was never my intent to fight again."

"But your father triggered you."

"My father will *always* trigger me." He glances over at me. "The good news is our exposure to him will be rare."

Our exposure. I like this phrase, but I focus on the content. I want to ask questions. For instance, why does his father blame him for his brother's death? But asking too much and giving too little doesn't seem fair or right. He gave this information to me, to ease me into a conversation about me, not him. And so, I say, "You're nothing like Brandon, Dash. And please don't misread what happened tonight. I would do anything with you."

"That's just it, Allie. You don't need to. We just need to do us. There's no such thing as too little or too much with me. Not with you. You're the only person who could step into hell with me and pull me out. You need to know that. And if you need me to pull you out, I will." He pauses for obvious emphasis and adds, "When you're ready."

"I *am* ready. I think seeing him, having him come at you like he did, just made him more present."

"Brandon," he says.

"Yes. Brandon. He triggered me. Your dad triggered you. All of this is a bad combination."

"Tell me all the reasons I want to beat his ass."

"You can't beat his ass or he wins."

"Not with my fists. I'm smarter than that, baby. That's why I keep the fighting underground. Tell me. What did he do to you?"

I turn away from him and when I would stand, Dash catches the blanket on either side of me and turns me to face him. "There is nothing you can't say to me," he says.

I could tell him the same applies to me, but that feels like me pushing him, and my gut says that's not what he needs right now. *Give trust. Get trust*, I think. I've kept too much from him, and if I hadn't, Brandon would never have become a problem. "All right. I'll tell you." I swallow hard and launch into my story. "My father had just come back into my life. I'd hungered for a relationship with him in ways I didn't realize until he showed up at my door. And Brandon is close to him, or was close to him. He introduced us. I think I fell for the idea of Brandon, and the new little family I'd have with him and my father, rather than actually for him."

"How did your mother feel about your father being back in your life?"

"She didn't know. She can't know, Dash. I don't know why I got so infatuated with the idea of my father. He was terrible to her. He was terrible to us. He just—he convinced me he had regrets, and he said he wanted to know his daughter."

"It's normal to want to know your parents, both of them. They're a part of you."

"He's not a part of me I want to claim."

"You know I understand. Tell me about Brandon."

"He wined and dined me and seemed really wonderful. Not your kind of wonderful, Dash. I never loved him. Like I said, it was the idea of him, so much so that I found out the hard way that I really didn't know him at all."

"What does that mean?"

"Not long after we were engaged, he'd had a bad day at the office. I was at his place and he—" I look away, my heart thrumming faster now. "He likes control and power. And I found out that meant while having sex."

Dash catches my chin and forces me to look at him. "What does that mean, Allie?"

"It means you aren't the first man to put a hand on my ass. I think that's why it surprises me that I like it when you do it."

"Did he hurt you?"

My fingers curl into my palms and my lashes lower. "Dash—"

"Allie," he says softly, insistently. "*Did he hurt you?*"

CHAPTER TWELVE

I pull away from Dash and stand up, wrapping the blanket around myself, giving him my back, and forcing myself to mentally travel to that night. I rotate to face Dash, who is still sitting on the bed as if he understands I need to be in control right now. I need space to achieve that control.

"He was drinking," I continue, "angry over a client who dropped him, and how much money he'd lose. He told me to undress. He wanted to watch. It felt very cold, kind of out of nowhere. We weren't kissing, or even talking. In fact, we were awkward because he was so damn agitated."

"And?" Dash prods.

"When I didn't want to do it, he got angry. He grabbed me and shoved me against the window, and told me *again* to undress. I did it because I was scared. I can't explain why, but I was scared. He'd never hurt me, but that night, I felt he was capable of such a thing."

"So you undressed," he assumes.

"Yes. And then he told me to get on my hands and knees."

Dash stands up and I hold out a hand. "Wait. Just let me get it all out. I did it. I knew I had to do it." I don't let myself linger on the words or even hold them inside. I just spit them out. "He spanked me and not gently, then he—he fucked me. When it was over, he told me the next time I dismiss him, he'd make it hurt worse." I laugh, but not with humor. "The next morning, he actually told me how hot that game we'd played had been."

"Allie," Dash says, but I cut him off.

"I'm not done, but I was done that night. I couldn't wait to get out of his apartment. When he left for work, I didn't call my father. I was ashamed. I didn't even go to work. I spent the day in Central Park, just walking and thinking. That night, I called him to break up with him, but he cut me off and told me he was working before I could get the words out. I couldn't let the relationship continue. I went to his office. I knew there were cameras and other people who would be working late. It felt safe. His secretary was gone and his door was open."

"What happened, Allie?"

"I heard him telling someone how he could fuck me any way he wanted, literally or otherwise. Turns out, he planned to marry me to inherit my father's money. My father knew, but my father just wanted to pry me out of my mother's hands and keep me close. I was Brandon's money card."

"What did you do?"

"I walked into his office, flung the ring at him, and told him he'd better cash it in because it's all the money he would get from me. I left then. I went to my father's apartment. Told him I knew everything, and that I never wanted to see him or Brandon again."

"But he keeps trying?"

"He did for a while. I thought that was over, and then he showed up in Nashville. I don't want my mother to deal with that right now. And I suddenly know how she feels when I coddle her. I don't want you to suddenly start thinking I'm going to freak out on you every time we get naked, Dash. I'm not."

Dash pushes to his feet and catches my hands. "I know. It's all about trust, which I'm going to do a better job of earning. Let's go back to the hotel. If you want to. Or we can stay here."

"No. I don't want to stay here. I didn't like feeling like this was home again."

His hand slides under my hair and he eases my gaze to his. "You have common sense, baby. I didn't want to have common sense. I didn't want you to be here, where you could stop me from fighting. But home always meant being with me."

"If you send me away again—"

"I will never be that foolish again." He captures my hand and kisses it. "How about a pizza, New York style?"

And just like that, Dash shuts the door on further conversation about his father. I know that's a problem. I'm sure he knows it, too. But I let it happen with good reason. I think it's just all too much right now: too much drama, too much pain, too much fighting, just *too much*.

LISA RENEE JONES

CHAPTER THIRTEEN

Once we're back at the hotel, Dash and I stuff our faces with pizza and without much ado, crash into the bed and each other. And how can we not? This Saturday has felt as if it lasted a week, not twenty-four hours. We wake Sunday morning, our bodies melded together, rain pitter-pattering on the window and my cellphone ringing. I groan and grab it from the nightstand to find my mother calling. "Mom?" I answer. "Why are you calling so early?"

"It's Sunday. You always get up early on Sunday."

Dash kisses my neck and says, "I'll order coffee."

"Tell Dash I said hello," my mother offers, as if him being in bed with me is old news.

"My mother says hello," I say, over my shoulder.

Dash calls out, "Morning, Mom," and rolls out of the bed.

Mom.

He called my mom, *Mom*.

"He called me Mom," my mother says. "Sounds like a man who plans on marrying you. Is there something I should know? You do need to get busy on making me some grandkids."

I sit up and watch Dash disappear from the bedroom into the living area in only a pair of pajama bottoms, naked from the waist up, muscles from here to Texas. "Let's not put the cart before the horse, Mother," I say, forcing my attention back to the call, and adding, "Your saying, not mine."

"All right then. How about Thanksgiving? Can I count on you both to be at our house?"

"I'll talk to Dash."

"Perfect. He can help put up the tree. Your stepfather's back is not what it used to be. How was the signing?"

"The fans love Dash," I say, avoiding the explosive parts of the day and night. "That was fun to experience."

"Was his father there? Did I read that? Did you meet him?"

"Yes. He was." I soften my voice. "Bad topic. He ranks right up there with my father."

"Oh no. I'm so sorry to hear that. What about his mother?"

"He lost her at a young age. She was the owner of Alice Home Shopping Network."

"What an interesting family, but oh my. A dad like yours but no mother to love him."

"He has a sister, Bella, who I'd like to invite to Thanksgiving as well."

"Please do. I'd love to meet her. All right, now I need to go make breakfast. When will you be home?"

"I'm not sure yet. I'll let you know."

By the time we disconnect, Dash is in the bathroom brushing his teeth. I glance at my messages to find several from Bella: *How is Dash?*

How are you?

Hello.

Hello?

Allie!

I reply with: *All is well. More later, probably when we get back. But we're okay. He is okay.*

Thank God, she says. *Thank God. When will you be back?*

I'll let you know when I know.

I set my phone aside and join Dash, claiming my toothbrush. Once our breath is fresh, Dash drags me between him and the counter to face him and he kisses me thoroughly before saying, "Yes to Thanksgiving. Where you go, I go. And as for Bella, I'm sure she'll say yes. And since she left me three messages, I'll call her. Do you want to ask her or me?"

"Maybe I should so she knows it's sincere?"

"I think she knows that already, but I think it would mean a lot coming from you."

"She's worried about what went down with your dad, Dash."

"I know, baby. Believe me, I know."

"What are you going to tell her?"

"The truth, as much as I dare tell her."

"She knows we had a fight, but nothing about the fight club."

His cellphone rings on the counter. He eyes the caller ID. "Speak of the devil herself."

I push to my toes and kiss him. "Talk to her."

I walk back into the bedroom and my phone is buzzing on the nightstand. So many calls, too little sunlight. I glance at the nine AM hour and decide it's still way too early for this. I pick it up and read the message, only to go cold. *This is your father. I know you're in the city. I think we should talk about Dash Black, among other things. I'll be at that little coffee shop you like at three o'clock.*

CHAPTER FOURTEEN

Dash is suddenly sitting next to me. "What's wrong, baby?"

I hand the phone to Dash and let him read the message. "He wants to talk about me, does he? Well, I say let's workout, eat, and then go talk to your father."

"Dash—"

"Baby, he is clearly not going away. And you don't have closure."

"And you do?"

"We're not talking about me."

I face him. "Maybe we should be."

"I'm not telling you we can't talk about me, or my father. We can. But right now, we're dealing with yours."

"I think we're dealing with yours, too."

"No. The last thing we have to deal with is my father. We avoid each other. We were tricked into that encounter."

"Because of Brandon."

"Which is not your fault," he assures me.

"What if this is Brandon at work again? What if he shows up?"

"Bring it," Dash says. "I'll be ready. The question is, will you? What if Brandon shows up?"

"I don't think he will, not with my father present."

"Unless that's not your father."

"You think it's Brandon?"

"After what happened at that book signing, I'd be prepared for anything."

My mind goes to the encounter between Tyler and Dash in the bar. That was intense and personal, I know, but isn't this as well?

"I think we should just skip the meeting. Or I need to go alone."

"I'd like to go," Dash says simply. "I think we should go together. But this isn't my decision to make. It's yours." He leans over and kisses me. "Think about it."

The idea that he's asked me rather than told me what should happen—and I sense he means this completely—matters to me. This is one of those moments when I love Dash all the more. He's dominant, controlling, even a tad bit arrogant, but he saves these things for the right times, usually when we're naked. Mostly. He has slips, but for the most part outside the bedroom, he's tender, caring, grateful.

"That doesn't mean I won't be nearby, like right outside the door, if you need me," he adds. "I told you, I'm protective, baby. I can't be any other way with you."

Another quality I like—no, love—about Dash. He really worries about me and while I know this partially comes from some of his deep-rooted pain and a history of loss, it still shows how much I mean to him.

"I need to call and deal with the pilot I have on standby to take us home," he continues. "When do you want that to be?"

"Tuesday? I just need to talk to my boss here tomorrow. Or even late tomorrow night."

"Tuesday morning," he says. "I'll arrange it. How about a workout and then lunch?"

"Only if there's coffee first."

"I'll order it now." He starts to get up.

I catch his arm. "What will you do if Brandon shows up?"

"I like control, Allie. Choosing to fight and randomly punching someone are two different things. He's in my world. I'm not in his world."

"He'll try and ruin you."

"Greater men, like my father, have tried and failed."

"Your father tried to ruin you?"

"A story better told over booze and when we're naked." He softens his voice. "But I'll tell you, Allie." He strokes my cheek and stands up, walking toward the bedroom door.

I glance down at the message again and reread it: *This is your father. I know you're in the city. I think we should talk about Dash Black, among other things. I'll be at that little coffee shop you like at three o'clock.* It doesn't sound like him and since I blocked his number, I can't even be sure it is him. I pull up his real number and unblock it. I shoot him a text: *Did you text me from another number about coffee today?*

He doesn't reply. I wait and wait. He still doesn't reply.

Nothing about this feels right.

And I know, *I just know*, that Brandon isn't done with us. I ran from him in the past. I know I did. But if there is one lesson I've learned this weekend, it's that running doesn't work. It just delays a problem and gives it time to grow bigger and bigger until it snowballs down the hill and crashes into you. I thought the crash had happened Saturday. But maybe that was just the start of a snowball. Trouble hasn't come and gone, it's still here.

LISA RENEE JONES

CHAPTER FIFTEEN

I freshen up and throw on my workout leggings and a tank top before heading out to the living room and kitchen area of the hotel suite. I find Dash standing by the window, a coffee cup in hand, still naked from the waist up. My stomach does this fluttery thing at the sight of him. That never happened with Brandon. Ever. I live with Dash now and I feel that just walking into the same room. I'm not sure that feeling will ever outstay its welcome. But people trying to get between us—that will, that has. First Tyler at the bar. Then Brandon. Then Dash's father. Now my father, or maybe it's not my father. I have no idea who that message was from.

Brandon, I think.

It has to be Brandon.

Which proves how little he knew me if he thinks my father is the person who can lure me to coffee.

Seeming to sense my presence, Dash turns to face me, his eyes lighting on me as if I light up his world the way he does mine. I know this is true, but there is this part of me, this insecure part of me, that struggles to see this reality when I know he loves me. A damaged, broken part of me I'd like to blame on Brandon, but the truth is, that's a lie I tell myself. I know, deep in my heart and soul, that I have to own how I allow myself to process life, how I allow events and people to affect me. I define my character. They do not.

"Coffee, at your service, cupcake," Dash announces, motioning to the pot on the table.

If he's upset over this thing with my father wanting to talk to me about him, he's not showing it. He joins me on the couch and pours my coffee, doctoring it to just the perfect place. He knows how much cream, how much Splenda. He knows me well and he hasn't known me long. *Because he tries*, I think. Dash actually wants to know what I like, so he puts in the effort to find out the little details that matter in ways I don't think I even realized until him.

I sip the warm beverage and say, "This is good, but I miss that coffee we started making at the apartment."

"You mean at home, baby?" he challenges softly.

My chest pinches with a kaleidoscope of emotion. "Yes. At home."

"You didn't want to call it that," he accuses softly. "We'll fix that, I swear, Allie."

"Dash—"

"We'll fix it." He clicks a few buttons on his phone and moves away from the emotional topic to our current situation with my father. "I know how your father knows you're in town and that we're together," he says, showing me an image of me and him together at the signing on what appears to be the Daily Report, a wildly popular news site with a celebrity section.

"My God, my hair is standing up," I say, cringing.

He laughs. "You look beautiful, baby. The point here is he knew we went public. We just forgot the obvious when talking about that text from your father."

"Or he's talking to Brandon again. Or it's Brandon himself texting me." I set my cup down. "But whatever the case, Dash, I realize now that pushing them away, shutting them out, was me trying to shut out my problems and not deal with them. I was running, and look where it got me. Look where it got us."

"No. You chose not to have them in your life, Allie. That's not running. That's a decision and one you were smart to make, considering what I now know."

"No matter how right or logical it seems, my state of mind is what ultimately matters. I was running, Dash. I wanted a new life. Granted, publishing was not as fulfilling as I'd expected it to be, but even my new job is, at least to some degree, a way to distance myself from the past. Though it's also an amazing opportunity and a place I've thrived."

"I was going to talk to you about that."

I twist around to face him. "I was going to talk to you about it, too."

"You want me to go first, or you first?"

"You," I say quickly, eager to know his point of view.

"Why don't we look for a place to live here in New York."

I blink. I mean, I know he referenced this in the past, but the idea that he would take action for me, uproot for me, blows me away. "You'd move for me?"

"Is that even a question?"

Last night, he told me to go home, and I'd thought he wanted me to go away. Now, he's offering to uproot his life for me. I lean over and kiss him on the cheek. He captures me and drags me closer, kissing me well and good before he says, "I'd do anything for you, Allie." His voice is low and rough with emotion. "Haven't you figured that out by now?"

I believe him. Because yes, he went to fight last night, but it's an addiction and he still left the fight for me. One day, it will be for him, too, I vow. I touch his face, love in that touch as I say, "I like being in Nashville." I sit up. "I need to tell you something. I need to tell you a lot of things about last night, Dash."

He arches a brow. "What about last night?"

"I called Tyler," I say quickly, "just to see if he knew where you would go here and of course, he didn't. I know you hate that and I'm sorry. I was worried. I was scared for you because of Brandon."

His lashes lower, his jaw clenching before he looks at me again. "I know you were."

That's all he says, *I know you were...*

CHAPTER SIXTEEN

I'm reminded of a quote I read once, though I can't say where I read it: *Honesty is the highest form of intimacy.* Last night, I felt the bond between myself and Dash shift and change, the bonds that were newly formed growing stronger. I know he is not pleased that I went to Tyler, but I can't allow that to stop me from speaking the words that linger on my tongue.

I've made the spur of the moment decision to tell Dash everything about last night, to protect him and us, and I'm not going to back down now. "I know you don't want Tyler involved in your life or mine," I quickly add, "but I also want honesty between us, Dash. I didn't tell you about Brandon, which you know why, but that blew up in my face. So, there's more to tell you and I'm just going to spit it out. When he couldn't help, I could think of only one other person who *might* help. Only one other person I knew who made a habit of discretion. That was Mark Compton, one of the owners of Riptide. I'm close to his mother who has cancer and who I'd hoped to visit while we were here. She's not up for it. But I know he'd help me because of how she feels about me. And I promised to connect his mother to my mother to talk about what they both are going through." I press my hand to my head. "I'm really rambling, but I'm just going to keep going. It turns out that Mark bets on the fights. He knew how to get me to you. And he wants his role with the underground fighting private as well. He told me about his bets so that I could tell you, and so I, we, knew he wouldn't burn you." I pause for his thoughts, but he says nothing, so I just keep on keeping on. "He also told me he wanted loyalty in exchange for help, but that he was clear that you came first before the job. I proposed an idea to keep the role I have now for Hawk Legal, but work for Riptide. He seems open to it."

Dash's cellphone rings and he glances at the number. "I need to take this and get changed." He stands up and he actually walks out of the room. I blink, confused first, and then concerned. I push to my feet and start to pace, not sure if I should follow him. He obviously wants a moment away from me. I walk to the window and stare out at the city I'd once thought a perfect place to live, but it was never the right place for me. I know that now.

My mind goes back to last night, and how perfect Dash's response to my inhibitions, my confessions about my past. I don't want him to feel betrayed by my actions when they were well-intentioned. I turn and race toward the bedroom. I find Dash at the window, much like I had been in the living room, his shoulders tensed. I don't even think twice. I rush toward him and then in a minute, I'm pushing in between him and the window, his fingers are in my hair and he's kissing me, a kiss that feels like ten thousand shades of torment.

"I'm sorry," he says when his mouth parts from mine. "I should never have put you in that position last night."

"I can't apologize for coming after you, Dash. I love you and—"

"I'm sorry," he repeats. "It won't happen again, Allie. I'm done fighting." He tilts my gaze to his. "I'm done fighting."

"It's not that easy, Dash. It's an addiction. I know you know that."

"I don't need that. I need you," he repeats. "I know I've said that before but you proved that to me last night. I thought I had to fight, and then you showed up, and I knew what a fool I was. Why was I there and not with

80

you? It won't happen again. If it's between you and fighting, you win."

"You need to do it for you, not me. You know that, right?"

"I'm doing it for both of us, baby."

But as Dash kisses me again, backing me toward the bed and undressing me, I know that nothing about what happened last night is as simple as this moment in his arms. Nor is it as simple as him choosing not to fight. Dash is captive to the past, just as I have been, and the past wants to destroy us. I still like to believe love conquers all. Of course, that sounds like a fairytale, but no one said fairytales don't include monsters.

It just means that in the end, the monsters are slain when a mighty battle is fought, but we survive.

LISA RENEE JONES

CHAPTER SEVENTEEN

Dash and I are on the treadmills, side-by-side, when a realization comes to me. I halt and look over at him. He punches his pause button and turns to look at me, both of us breathing heavily. "What, baby?"

"You didn't involve me in a solution last night and look where we ended up."

"I told you that won't happen again."

"I know. I'm not talking about you. I'm talking about me. I need to involve you in my solution. I want you to go with me to the coffee shop today."

His hand covers my hand on the arm of my machine, and he says, "Good. I want to go with you, but I can sit outside or at another table and be close if you need me. That's not excluding me, Allie. There's no right or wrong answer to how you handle this. There's just what feels like the best move and that has to come from your gut."

"Yes," I say. "Good advice. Thank you. Let's run."

He nods, and we both return to our workouts, my mind replaying so many moments in my past with my father. I never really gave him the chance to tell his side of the story, but then, he never really made an effort, either. And if that is him who's been texting me, why won't he answer his phone? I actually tried to call him on both numbers, the one he—or someone—texted me with, and the one I know to be his. A part of me prays my father is the one contacting me. The same part of me that wants him to show support for Dash after all that happened with Brandon. The little girl in me who still craves her father. If this is him, he is going to disappoint me again, but at least I will sit face-to-face with him and

83

tell him how I feel. Something I was too cowardly to do in the past.

By the time I end my run and Dash does the same, I've made a decision. Dash and I step off our machines and I turn to look at him. "I'm done running. I'm *really* going to go to the coffee meeting, no matter who shows up."

He touches my cheek. "I know, baby. I'm surprised you didn't."

There is a reason Dash and I were drawn to each other from the moment we met. We both look into the mirror and try not to see the truth, but when we look at each other, we see clearly. It's funny how one person can shine a light on the darkness in our souls. I step forward and wrap my arms around Dash. "We can go early so you can write."

"I was thinking more we could go get naked to work off your nerves."

"We already did that," I remind him, smiling. He makes me smile and I love that about Dash.

He arches a brow. "And?"

"You have a book to finish," I chide. "You're going to have me, Bella, and Ghost angry if you don't finish it on time. Not to mention a legion of fans."

"You're a slave driver, woman, but yes. I do have a book to write. And if you want to go early, we'll go early. And together."

"Yes," I say softly. "That's what I'm telling you, Dash. I don't need you to sit outside the coffee shop or at another table. Together."

He strokes my hair behind my ear, a gentle touch that swims through my senses, and says, "Always, Allie."

"And if Brandon shows up instead of my father?"

"I'll beat his ass, of course."

My eyes go wide. "Dash—"

He laughs. "I told you. That's not how I play this game."

"Then how do you play it?"

"Like I'm Ghost."

"You want to kill him."

"Not literally, baby. But I have a plan."

"And that plan is?"

"To sic Bella on him," he laughs, scooping me up in his arms. "All other questions must be asked naked in the shower."

In other words, no more questions, but I'm laughing as he carries me through a public gym. A woman snaps our pictures and murmurs something about Dash Black. Good Lord, I have bad hair again. And for a man who likes to keep a low profile, he's not keeping a low profile.

But maybe the shower is exactly where I demand a promise that he doesn't beat Brandon's ass. Even if I wish he could.

LISA RENEE JONES

CHAPTER EIGHTEEN

Dash and I dress warmly—me in blue jeans and a violet sweater, Dash in all black—before we walk to lunch. Another short walk and we arrive at the coffee shop. With two hours to spare before the meeting with my father, or perhaps Brandon, we order our coffees and open our MacBooks. It's a familiar thing for us now, being beside each other, working, just being together.

"If Brandon shows up, don't beat him up, Dash. He'll try to provoke you."

Dash's lips curve. "Well, it's nice to know you know how easily I could beat your ex's ass, but that would be so easy that it wouldn't be much of a challenge. Or very satisfying. I prefer to beat him at a different game."

"Which is what?"

He catches my hand and kisses it. "Keeping you."

I warm with this sweet statement, but Dash is too nonchalant about the Brandon thing. "What are you up to, Dash Black?"

"Me? Up to something?"

"Don't play coy."

It's at that moment that a man walks up to our table and says, "Are you Dash Black? God, man, I love your books."

Two more people follow him, and then another. It's a steady trail of people and Dash is humble and generous with his time. When we're finally alone again, I say, "I love how you are. Just so you know. All of you. Even the broken parts, Dash."

His eyes darken, a sharp spark of emotion in their depths before he shoves whatever I've made him feel away, and teases, "You're the glue to my glass, baby," and then softly adds. "And I love how you are, too."

"I don't want to come back here, Dash. I know I told you I did, but I don't. And it's not about running. Not this time."

"I know that, baby, or I wouldn't let it happen."

His phone buzzes with a text message and he glances at the message, his lips twitching slightly before he glances up at me. "Bella's dad is driving on Thanksgiving, so she's coming to Thanksgiving dinner with one condition—we watch him race."

"I forget all about her father when I shouldn't do that. I know she's close to him. I don't even know where he lives."

"He has a place in Nashville and North Carolina. North Carolina is where most of the drivers live, which is why it's nicknamed Race City, USA."

"I see. I feel bad that I've ignored that part of her life, but I'm excited that she's coming. I have to tell my mom. She is going to be so happy. It will be like a big family Thanksgiving."

Dash's lips curve. "Yes, it will, baby, and I for one have not had one of those in a very long time. Neither has Bella. She often goes to the track, but this year she said she really would like to stay in Nashville. I had a feeling she'd feel that way. She loves her father, but his career makes it hard for them to have quality time together."

"I'm really glad she's coming. What do you normally do?"

"Go with her when I can."

I lean over and kiss his cheek. "I'm thrilled to have you both with me. And my mom will be, too. I'm going to call her outside so I don't keep you from writing. And because she will squeal so loudly the whole coffee shop will hear."

He laughs and I stand up, sliding on my coat as I hurry toward the door.

I shouldn't step outside into a cold day, but I don't care, I'm too eager to talk to my mother. I step to the left of the door, as the sidewalk bustles with people, horns honking, voices lifting in what is just another day in Manhattan. It has a life of its own, but the thing is, so does Nashville. Sometimes we push back on what is comfortable and safe as boring. Our soul seeks growth and adventure therefore we spread our wings and fly far away, only to return home to discover it's always been the place happiness blooms. I blossomed in New York. I bloomed when I returned to Nashville.

With Dash.

"Allie," my mother answers. "Oh my God, I just saw the photos of you and Dash. You looked beautiful and he is such a looker."

I laugh. "Yes. Yes, he is. And my hair was standing up."

"I didn't notice. I just saw your beauty."

"And I love you for it, Mom. I do."

"I guess you two are pretty official now, huh?"

"How's this for official?" I ask. "Dash and his sister are coming for Thanksgiving. They're looking forward to a family dinner."

"That is fabulous. Oh my. It will be a big family holiday. But oh my," she says again. "I mean, our house is very humble. I'm sure Dash's place, I mean your place now, too, is gorgeous—which I'd like to see by the way—but should we have it there?"

My place with Dash. God, I love how real that is, how much more real after this weekend, it somehow feels. But as to her worry, I say, "Dash has never once made me feel like your home was anything but perfect, Mom. I think the very idea that it's your home is what makes it special."

"You're sure?"

"Absolutely, but when we get back you should come over."

"I'd love that."

We chat a few more minutes and the chill starts to overcome me. "I'll call you later, Mom. I'm outside in New York. It's freezing. Dash is inside a coffee shop working."

"Get back to your man. I love you."

"I love you, too."

I disconnect quickly and try to call my father again. When he doesn't answer, I text him. Next, I dial the number that texted me earlier, but once again to no avail. I send a text. I wait a moment in hope of a reply, and that's when that strange vibe of being watched that I had back in Nashville returns. Instantly uneasy, my gaze lifts left, right, and all around. There are just so many people and windows above us across the street in the buildings, that I can't really be sure the sensation is for not. Maybe it's Brandon, sizing us up before he makes a move. Then again, this feeling started in Nashville. It's then that I realize that I haven't thought of Allison in days. I wonder who has, if anyone? She seems to be fairly alone in the world. I think about myself, and how few people I had in my life before Dash and Bella.

I make a vow then that when I get back to Nashville, I'll find her.

For now, the creepy feeling of being watched won't go away, and I hurry back inside the coffee shop.

CHAPTER NINETEEN

The definition, per Websters, for anticipation is rather simple.

1: excitement about something that's going to happen She looked forward to the trip with anticipation. 2: the act of preparing for something.

Obviously, Webster keeps things pretty simple. Anticipation is more than excitement or the act of preparing for "something." First of all, anticipation isn't always about excitement. Sometimes it's about dread or nervousness or uncertainty. It's the act of expecting "something" to happen and having that expectation become a living, breathing entity all in and of itself.

Waiting for my three o'clock coffee date is that and more. All of those things wrapped up in one big ball of energy that seems to ping pong through my body. At a quarter until three, Dash shuts his MacBook and says, "Too bad this meeting isn't in a bar instead of a coffee shop, because clearly you need a shot."

"You do remember how badly I drink, right?"

"With the amount of caffeine in you right now, I think a little booze wouldn't hurt you one little bit."

"I'm not sure either of us wants to see that version of me with my father or Brandon."

His lips curve. "I think it could be rather amusing, at least with Brandon."

"I might qualify for a character in a horror movie in that situation." I glance at the time on my phone. Ten more minutes. "I'm nervous."

Dash leans closer. "Why?"

"I don't want you to fight—"

"Already covered. I'm not going to fight. What else?"

I draw a breath on the difficult admission I force myself to speak. "Brandon will try to humiliate me in front of you."

"Impossible. And Brandon will be focused on me. It's a guy thing. It's a power thing."

"He likes power as much as you do."

"Liking it and owning it are two different things, baby. You should know that by now."

He's right again. "I do," I say. "He demands it. You own it."

His eyes warm with approval, his voice softening. "Then stop worrying."

"If my father shows up, and you're here, he won't be confrontational. That's not how my father operates. He uses his fame to seduce people. I'm not sure how he'll handle you. You're more famous than he is."

"I'm more concerned with how he handles *you*, Allie. You're his daughter. I'd like to think he'd fight for you."

"I think the problem is that he did, and he showed his character in doing so, but the truth is, I never gave him the chance to explain himself. I was angry and assumed he did everything as Brandon said he did, and Brandon isn't exactly a reliable source. But he didn't deny anything. And he didn't stop me when I left. He didn't fight for me then, but maybe I hurt him when I assumed his guilt."

"He showed up at that party at Tyler's house. Maybe he wanted to talk."

"And yet, the message he sent me wasn't about me, or that, but rather you."

"That could be an excuse to see you."

I glance at the time again and then the door. "It's three now," I say. "Why isn't he, or someone else, here?"

Dash captures my hand under the table. "It's going to be okay. You're facing this. That's a good thing."

"It's closure," I say. "I think it's necessary." I hesitate and ask, "Did you ever get that with your father?"

"Sometimes closure is truly accepting there is nothing you can do to change a situation. In that regard, yes, I have closure. Nothing will change for me with my father. I don't want him in my life. I know that. You don't about yours."

Dash's words linger with me as the minutes tick by. At three-thirty, I dial my father, but he doesn't answer. I text him. I text the number that someone claiming to be him texted me with, all for naught. At three forty-five, I turn to Dash. "Let's go see my father. Let's go to his apartment."

Dash packs up his MacBook and with no hesitation, says, "Let's go."

"He lives near Central Park. It's a pretty good hike, but I think I need to walk and think."

He lifts both of our bags on his broad shoulder. "Then we'll walk."

A few minutes later, we're maneuvering through the hustle and bustle of the busy New York sidewalks, and my mind isn't filled with the fretting I'd expected. I'm resolved, dogmatic in my determination to embrace closure. I'm reminded of something Queen Compton told me once. I'd been fretting about a man who'd been forced to sell a cherished item.

"As the great Roman philosopher, Seneca, said, 'Every new beginning comes from some other beginning's end.' No one ever said an ending or a new beginning had to be easy to be the right thing to do. In fact, the harder the change, the bigger the reward. Seems to me that not only sums up your customer's situation, but your recent change of career."

She was talking about the massive payday that client ended up pocketing and, of course, my career move from publishing to Riptide. And while she's too sick to offer advice now, her influence is stronger than ever. I swear she's whispering those same words to me now. "Every new beginning comes from some other beginning's end," and they ring truer than ever. But an ending translates to a conclusion. If I want to move on in my life, to let go of my baggage and start fresh with Dash in Nashville, there is no running away. I have to walk away from this life decisively and *with closure*.

CHAPTER TWENTY

Dash and I reach my father's fancy Central Park building and pause at the security desk, where Kevin, the tall, dark-haired man with lined, friendly eyes, greets me. Kevin has been in his position for so long he probably knows my father better than I do. "Well, well, Ms. Allie," he says warmly. "Good to see you back around." He glances at Dash and then me. "Seems you surround yourself with famous people and still manage to shine brightly. You look lovely as usual." He eyes Dash again. "And you, sir, are brilliant. I love me some Ghost."

Dash smiles and shakes his hand. "And you, sir, are right about her. She does shine brightly and she does look lovely."

"Okay, you two, flattery is not necessary, but thank you both. Is he here, Kevin?"

"I'm afraid not, honey. He's just left for Europe for some international sporting event he's commentating. I'll chide him for not telling you when he returns. And I'm quite certain he'd enjoy meeting Dash Black."

I draw in a breath. "Thanks, Kevin. Yes. We're leaving soon, so I thought we'd catch him."

"I'll tell him you came by."

I nod and turn to Dash. Dash offers Kevin a folded bill I assume to be large, because this is Dash, as he says, "Please don't. We have a surprise in mind."

"Oh, of course," Kevin replies, but he waves off the bill. "You don't have to pay me. I'm happy to stay out of what is none of my business."

"All the more reason I want you to take it," Dash says. "Not very many people are that honorable. Please. Happy holiday season."

Right about then, someone walks by in a fairy costume, and I realize it's actually Halloween.

Kevin doesn't notice. He's focused on Dash. He hesitates, but finally accepts the tip. "Thank you, sir. That is greatly appreciated."

"Thanks, Kevin," I say.

"You're very welcome. I'm just glad to see you come back around again."

"Happy holiday season," I say, trying to keep my voice perky, but the reality of the situation is starting to hit me. Today is not about conclusions and closure. My father didn't contact me. Someone else did. That someone is probably Brandon, who vowed revenge on me through Dash. The minute Dash and I are outside, amid the crazy wash of the people-paved walkway, we instinctively take a few steps to the right of the busy doorway, I turn to face him. We're almost taken out by a woman wearing a witch hat and we instinctively move away from the door and near the wall. His hands come down on my shoulders and he says, "I love you."

Those three words don't have the impact he wishes for. "And I love you, too, which is exactly why I cannot allow Brandon to hurt you."

"I'm not that easy to hurt, Allie."

"But you're human, Dash, even if you don't like to admit it. And you're high-profile. You have a big ol' target on your forehead. He knows about your fighting. I know he knows. It was something he said, it was how cocky he was, the way he baited you."

He captures my hand. "Come. I'm going to make you feel better." He starts walking, taking me with him.

I tug on his arm, halting him. "Dash, I'm serious," I state, the minute he rotates back to me. "This is a problem. He's a problem."

"Which is why we're going back to the hotel, where I'm going to let you in on my plan, which I wanted to make come together before I shared with you. But it has. We're there now." He motions toward the SUV. "Are you in?"

"Tell me now. Please. I'm losing my mind with worry."

"At the hotel, baby. I can't properly make you appreciate this plan on the street or in a vehicle with a driver in front."

"You're killing me."

"Softly, I promise." He's already walking, leading me to the SUV where our driver awaits.

On the ride back to our hotel, traffic is hell, slow as snails, and I can't take it. Dash reads my mood and has the driver drop us several blocks away from our destination, allowing us to finish our travel by foot. When finally, we're inside our room and have discarded our coats, Dash motions for me to join him on the couch. He opens his briefcase, removes his MacBook, sets it on the coffee table, and lifts the lid. Once he's keyed it to life and punched a few buttons, he turns the screen for me to view. My lips part with a headline that reads: *Dash Black's Late Nights in the Seedy World of Underground Fight Clubs.* My eyes go to his. "Keep reading," he urges.

In a secret storyline for his next Ghost novel, the international bestseller of the Ghost Assassin series has been spending time in the secret underground world where fighters fight without rules. The former FBI agent turned author confesses to actually fighting himself in these clubs, to ensure his story is as vividly real to life as he can possibly deliver.

In a phone interview with Dash Black, this reporter got to pick his brain and try to peel away the mystery of the oh-so-private man behind the wildly popular

Ghost novels. While I didn't reveal anything shocking, I did manage a few rather candid moments. Here were my ten rapidfire questions and Dash's surprising answers:

Who is the new woman in your life?

The only woman in my life is Allie Wright, who I'm only naming because if I don't, some reporter will stalk us until I do. She's beautiful, kind, smart. She's a former editor for a New York publisher. She's also the only person I've ever given a sneak peek of a novel.

As if he senses the part I'm on, he says, "This hasn't been published. It hits tomorrow morning. If you want your name removed—"

I face him. "No." My heart swells with the open way he proclaims us together. "What you said about me was *everything,* Dash. But are you sure you want to talk about your fighting?"

"It's the only thing anyone can use against me, Allie. That means Brandon. This scoops his story. And Bella talked to the creative team for the TV show and they love the story. They think it can be used to promote the series."

"Which lands where?"

"I'm still negotiating. Maybe Paramount. Maybe Netflix. We'll see."

I glance at the headlines again, and while I can see now how this protects Dash, and even makes him more interesting than he already is to the public, I'm not sure it achieves his goal of getting rid of Brandon.

"This won't make him go away," I say, glancing back at him. "All it does is force him to sidestep. And the longer he waits to attack, the angrier he will become."

"Oh, he's angry right about now, I'm sure," he replies dryly. "Because so was my sister and my father. Bella tried to get Brandon fired today. It was too late. My father made that happen."

I twist around even further to fully face Dash. "*Fired*?"

"Fired. My father is a powerful man in publishing."

"Getting fired is fuel on the inferno. Brandon will go after you and your dad."

"And that would be stupid. I frankly don't know why he was foolish enough to think my father wouldn't react firmly to the stunt he pulled with that signing. I suspect his anger will be directed at him, not us, and perhaps turn the flames in my father's direction."

I open my mouth to protest, but he holds up a finger. "He won't get the chance to attack my father or us. Brandon's going to get a very lucrative offer to work in a European publishing office. There's no way he'll decline."

"This feels *too good* for him. And even so, how can we even be sure he accepts the offer? He's a real football and apple pie kind of guy."

"Neil was able to easily find dirt on him. Brandon will discover just how much he needs to leave the country tomorrow."

"What kind of dirt?"

"I'd rather you not know in case you ever have to testify to that effect."

My hand goes to my neck. "Good Lord. I almost married him. How bad is it?"

"Dirty and ugly. But it works for us. This plan, this solution, works out well for him and us. He leaves. We get rid of him. And while I'd prefer to let him wallow in his fear after finding out he's been exposed, while freaking out over what comes next, I want him out of our lives now, not later. We can choose war or peace, Allie. I choose peace for our sake, not for his. If he still chooses war, the gloves are off and I promise you my bare-knuckle brawl is better than his."

The problem with this statement is that he's convinced this will never come to that. I, on the other hand, am not. Brandon's devious. He's the devil. I'm not sure he'll leave the country. Will Dash win a war? Yes. Will Brandon hurt him in the process? He might, and that's my fear.

CHAPTER TWENTY-ONE

*"The greater our knowledge increases the more our
ignorance unfolds."*
–John F. Kennedy

That quote was in a high-profile book I once edited
on the history of the presidency. To me, this translates
as a willingness to be dumb and blind, and therefore, we
have an excuse for being ignorant. It's a form of hiding,
as is running. I decide that the only way to quell my fears
over Brandon lashing out at Dash is either by way of time
passing without trouble ensuing, or by arming myself
with knowledge, which I've always considered a form of
power. Therefore, I focus on knowledge.

I read Dash's entire interview, starting with the
rapidfire questions.

Q: What, or who, inspired Ghost?

*A: My work experience, a love for movies, books,
and an obsession with both the Bond movies and
Dexter. Bond is a larger-than-life character, but he is
almost too perfect, and a bit sterile, an emotionless
machine. Dexter, on the other hand, IS emotionless.
He's a killer, after all, but somehow the writers make
you root for him. That's brilliance. When you can make
a viewer root for a killer, you've honed your craft.*

He's absolutely accurate and he could be speaking of
himself. Dash has honed his craft. He created Ghost, an
assassin, a cold-blooded killer, and managed to make us
all root for him. That requires a gift, a magical way of
crafting words. He's a warrior with a pen, but he's also a
warrior for those he loves. And yet, his father would have
us all believe he all but shoved his brother behind the

wheel of a car and forced him to drive drunk. I will never believe such a thing.

Ever.

I move on to the next question and forget about seeking knowledge to fight Brandon. The next question is: *What scares you, Dash?*

A: Mushrooms. They're disgusting.

It's a slick answer that is no answer at all. *Death* scares him, and not his own.

I keep reading, and by the time I'm done, I recognize how much Dash's words, both dictated, written, and spoken, speak to me beyond the surface. I understand him. I know him beyond what I'd know of any other person I knew for the exact amount of time.

I don't realize how long I've been absorbed in a short-written interview until Dash sets a cup of coffee in front of me. "Thank you," I say, glancing over at him.

"Any suggestions?"

"None. You handle reporters with the same finesse you have in writing a book. How in the world did you make this happen so quickly?" I ask.

"Bella," he says. "I mentioned being willing to bare-knuckle brawl. She's a pretty good bare-knuckle brawler herself. But my father's predictability helped. I knew he wasn't behind that bullshit signing. I also knew he wouldn't let Brandon get away with setting us up, either. As for the rapidfire speed to go along with the rapidfire questions, I did the interview all on text and email today at the coffee shop."

He jumped through hoops, and guilt stabs at me. "Thank you, Dash. And I'm sorry again about all of this. I should have dealt with him properly and none of this would have happened."

"You have nothing to thank me for or apologize for, Allie. As for Brandon, you owed that little bastard nothing but goodbye. This isn't your mistake, it's his, which is why he's about to get the shit scared out of him. He's not your father. The two situations are not the same."

"They're both things I ran from. I didn't finish the story."

"Yes, you did. You wrote the ending. He tried to change it. What would you have done differently with Brandon?"

"Besides never saying yes to anything with him?" I ask, without expecting an answer. "I don't know," I add. "I guess nothing."

"Exactly," he replies. "He blamed you for foiling his plan to use you. That's on him, not you. When there's a snake coming at you, you cut off his head. That's what you did."

"No," I correct. "That's what *you're* doing."

"You had no reason to believe an ending wasn't an ending with him. On the other hand, you do with your father. You don't feel right about how you ended your relationship with him. Does he deserve another chance to make things right with you? If you truly don't know the entire story about what happened between him and Brandon, then maybe. I don't know. And neither do you right now. You want to know and that's what matters."

"Are you comfortable with how things ended with your father, Dash?"

His fingers flex where they rest on my leg. "You know he blames me for my brother's death. There's really no coming back or together from that for either of us."

I remembered the look on his father's face when he looked at Dash and it was nothing short of contempt. So many words come to my tongue, only to be swallowed before spoken. I settle on, "I want to ask questions. You know I want to ask questions."

His chin lifts, his gaze reaching for the sky right through the ceiling before he meets my stare, and he lets me see the pain in his eyes as he says, "Like my father, my brother had a drinking problem that escalated when he joined me at college. I was young. I thought it was just the whole college party thing, but it grew tiresome. I babysat him all the damn time. That night we were at the same party. I'm the older brother. He got behind the wheel. And the only person who hates me more than I hate myself for letting that happen is my father."

And therefore, he punishes himself, in a fight club and with someone else's fist, and of course, that need for pain is driven by his admitted self-hate. As for his father, he could have helped Dash move forward from the loss, he could have loved the son he has left on this earth, and held him close. Instead, he shoved a blade into his heart and that blade cuts him over and over again.

I climb onto Dash's lap, straddling his hips, and press my hands to his handsome face. "You are not to blame and I will tell you that over and over if that's what it takes to make you forgive yourself."

He rolls me to my back and settles on top of me, his breath warm, his body hard. "For how many days, Allie?"

"What does that mean, Dash?" I whisper.

"For a month? For a year? For three years? For the *rest of your life*? Because this is not going away. Ever, Allie. It's *not* going away."

But he thinks I will. That's what he's telling me. And I'm not sure anything but full disclosure about what created his father's accusations and his guilt, which he hasn't yet given me, will convince him otherwise.

CHAPTER TWENTY-TWO

Because this is not going away.

With Dash still on top of me, his mouth a breath from mine, those words radiate between us. *"This"* I am certain is not just the death of his brother, but his own self-hate, his *guilt*.

I barely have time to digest the darkness in those words before he's kissing me, ravenous, hungry, *tormented*. I kiss him back, trying to answer a question it feels like he's asking, without ever asking it. Will I stay? Will I still love him if I know everything about that night his brother died because I don't yet? My fingers dive into his hair, my body arches against his. A rush of heat and need overcomes us, consuming us. His emotions are a current tugging me under, and I drown in them, live in them, feel them in every way possible. I am lost in Dash and I barely know how we end up naked. He touches me all over, his hand settling on my breast, fingers on my nipple, his cock thick and hard between my legs, pressing into the slick, wet heat of my sex.

I gasp with the feel of him entering me, and gasp again as he drives hard and deep, and sensations rocket through me. What follows is nothing that I have ever known with Dash or any other man. It's fucking. It's lovemaking.

We move together, we sway together, we *grind* and *pant* and *demand* from each other. Every touch is fire. Every move is wicked. Every sensation greater than the one before it. I crave the moment I shatter. I dread the moment this is over. And yet it must end and before I can delay that inevitable, I shatter, the low groan of Dash's pleasure melding with my own. Time stands still until my body relaxes into the cushion, and he shifts slightly to rest his weight on his side, but stays on top of me.

"I don't want children, Allie. You need to know that." He pulls back to look at me. "That won't change."

We've gone for torment and guilt every day of our lives to kids and he expects a negative reaction. "I've never even thought about having kids, Dash."

He grabs a tissue from the box on the end table, offering it to me before he pulls out and sits up, but he stays right there, elbows on his knees. I clean up and pull a blanket around my shoulders, and sit next to him. "One day you'll think about kids, Allie."

My stomach flip flops and not in a good way. "Why do I feel like you're looking for a reason to leave, Dash?"

He glances over at me. "I'm trying to make you happy."

"You make me happy. I come from a broken home, Dash. I love my mother, but she pined for my father, and it affected my childhood. I'm not thinking about my biological clock."

He presses his lips together and looks away. "My father and brother are alcoholics. I control it with physical activity, I rarely overindulge in alcohol, but I'm fucked up. I know this." He looks at me again. "Too much to be a father."

"This isn't an issue."

"Did you talk about kids with Brandon?"

"Actually, no. We never talked about kids."

"If I put you in a room with my father, he'd make you hate me."

He is naked in every way, exposed, vulnerable, and still affected by that encounter between me and his father at the signing. "Never."

"You're wrong."

"Then why don't you put me in a room with your father and find out?"

He drapes his arm around me and pulls me close, his hand on my face, tilting my gaze to his. "Because I don't want you to hate me."

My heart squeezes with the rawness of his tone. "You do enough of that for the whole planet, Dash. You think I haven't conjured up ideas about what happened and why you feel guilty? I'm still here, Dash. I'm not going anywhere. I can handle this. I promise."

"Until you can't."

"Don't do that. Not to me and not to yourself."

"I'm never telling Bella what happened that night. He was my father and stepmother's son. She wasn't close to him. What she did to help him was for me and because she's a good person. She doesn't need to know."

"I won't tell her," I vow. "That's between you and her, Dash. I will never break your trust."

"I know that but Allie, I'm just not ready to tell you everything."

He didn't say, "I'm never telling you," which is more than I expected. I press my hand to his face and say, "I know and it's okay. Maybe one day you will. Maybe you won't." I stop myself there, though I really want to tell him that I can't fully help him cope with whatever he feels if I don't understand where those emotions come from.

"One day," he says softly.

"Let's go home," is my reply. "I'll call Mark and talk to him about my job and then let's just go home."

"God, yes," he replies. "Let's go home. I'll arrange our flight."

CHAPTER TWENTY-THREE

"After all this time, I know exactly where I belong."
—Meg Rosoff

The day I arrived in New York City, my eyes were filled with the wonders of a city that was all bright lights, opportunity, and adventure, a place I was now to call home. Today, the day I will soon leave and no longer call it home, I feel no regret. Not for coming. And not for my decision to leave. Do I hope that my career with Riptide might find a lifeline? Yes. Very much. Will I choose Riptide over Nashville, where both Dash and my mother live? No. No, I will not.

If happiness is where the heart is and my heart is no longer in New York City.

It's in Nashville.

As John Denver sang, *"Country roads, take me home, To the place where I belong."*

My suitcase is open on the bed and I've all but finished packing when Dash enters the bedroom as he sticks his phone back in his pocket. "I already had a pilot on the payroll for the next few days. We're meeting him at the airstrip. I told him we need at least three hours. I thought you might want to swing by your apartment and get a few things." He glances at his watch. "That's still going to put us home pretty late. I'd say nine with no delays."

"I'll just let the movers get the rest of my stuff here. As for the time, I'm okay with that if you're okay with that. I'd just like to be home."

He stops on the opposite side of the bed. "What about your job, Allie?"

"I do need to call Mark, but they're not counting on me for Riptide business. I was just going in to work on the valuations for the auction, but really, it can all be finished by phone."

"You're sure?"

"Yes," I laugh. "I'm sure. Stop worrying. This city has not been kind to me, Dash. The only good thing here has been Riptide and maybe I can keep that job somehow. Which is why I need to call Mark. I told him he'd see me tomorrow." I walk to the nightstand and grab my phone.

"We can stay, Allie. Don't leave early because of me. We're okay, *we're good,* no matter where we are."

"I know," I say. "But that's all the more reason I want to go home. Home feels different and this isn't my home anymore, Dash."

He rounds the bed and steps close, his woodsy masculine scent warming me as much as his hand cupping my face. "Are you one hundred percent sure?"

"Yes." I cover his hand with mine. "Nashville is good for my soul. And so are you and my mother."

"All right then," he says, kissing me. "Call your boss. I'll pack."

"Good. Hurry. I'm starving. Let's get something to eat before we get on the plane."

"I would love a New York slice before we leave."

"I know a spot," I assure him.

"I'm sure you do," he says, stepping away from me to walk into the bathroom.

Feeling a little shy about talking to Mark about Dash in front of Dash, I walk into the living area and pull on my coat before stepping onto the balcony. I punch in Mark's number and he answers on the first ring. "Ms. Wright. I heard he didn't fight."

"You heard right."

"Good thing I didn't bet."

I get to the point. "I'm going back to Nashville."

"I assumed as much. I'm in my office. Come see me before you fly out."

My heart thunders in my chest. He wants me to come there now? This can't be good. "How long will you be there?"

"How soon can you be here?"

"Thirty to forty-five minutes." And when I open my mouth to ask if I'm about to be fired, he says, "See you then."

He disconnects.

"Damn it."

"What does that mean?"

I whirl around to find Dash standing in the doorway and I suddenly realize I'm cold, really cold. "He wants me to come to the office on our way out of town. I'm pretty sure I'm being fired. Or not. I don't know. I'm not sure he would have me come by to fire me, but then again, Mark Compton is not afraid of confrontation."

"Well, I'm packed if you're packed. Let's go see Mark." He backs up and I follow him back into the room.

"You want to see Mark?" I ask urgently, not sure where this is going. "Why?"

"Mark did me a favor last night. He got you to me. And I needed that. We needed that. I owe him."

"I'm not sure I want you to be there when I get fired, Dash."

"He's not firing you. You've decided to leave. He wouldn't give you the time of day if he didn't want to change your mind."

"You think?"

"I do. And if he does, we'll find a place here."

"He won't."

"We'll see."

"Okay," I say, "but I'd rather eat pizza after the meeting, so I know if I'm pigging out to celebrate or to console myself."

CHAPTER TWENTY-FOUR

Dash and I arrive at the Riptide offices thirty-five minutes later.

The security guard meets us at the door and allows our entry. After we rid ourselves of our coats, leaving them upfront, I motion Dash in the direction we'll be headed. "I'll show you to the break room. There's coffee and cocoa and just about anything else you could want."

"Why don't you show me to Mark's office?" he says, catching my hand and walking me to him. "I really do want to thank him."

"Why do I feel like it's more?"

"Because everything about us is more, Allie."

Okay, he's not wrong about that. He's really not. Everything with this man is more than I ever imagined, which is why I'm here about to quit my job. The door behind us opens in a gust of wind and I turn to find Mark, looking oh so arrogantly Mark, even in casual wear and a sleek leather jacket. In other words, composed, dominant and demanding. His very presence assumes all the energy in the room turns toward him.

He greets the doorman and then saunters a few steps in our direction to greet us. "Dash Black," Mark murmurs, glancing at me and then Dash again. "I didn't expect to see you here."

"Dash knows you helped me, Mark. I ended up telling him."

Mark arches a brow at me, those arrogant gray eyes of his seeing everything, and telling nothing. His lips twitch slightly, and his gaze shifts back to Dash. "You clearly don't want to kick my ass, but you do want to size me up. I'm a man who appreciates privacy," he states. "Yours and mine."

"Unfortunately," Dash replies, "Allie's ex, does not."

"A dangerous quality in a man who lives to cause trouble," Mark comments.

"Which is why I am choosing a preemptive strike rather than a reactive one," Dash replies. "Tomorrow morning there will be an interview exposing my fight club research for the next Ghost novel."

Mark's lips quirk. "Knock the wind right out of his sails. I like it. I do have a file of information on the ex, just in case, he's a problem. You might find it worth a look." He motions toward the offices. "Let's go sit down and chat."

I'm stunned in that moment to realize that Mark Compton cared enough about all of this to actually try and help.

We follow Mark to his office and gather around a small conference table. Mark slides a file toward Dash, a file already on the table, almost as if he expected him to visit. Dash opens it and flips through the pages before glancing at Mark. "While I already know this information, I'm curious why you do." Dash slides the file toward me, his attention remaining on Mark.

Mark's answer comes without hesitation. "If Brandon is looking to stir up trouble for Allie, he could shift his attention to her employment, and therefore, my operation. He has to be dealt with. Furthermore, Allie has my mother's favor. That means she has mine."

"How is she?" I ask.

"She's a warrior," he replies. "And she's putting up a good fight. She'll be happy to know you are as well."

"I appreciate what you did last night," Dash interjects. "And for your discretion. I owe you one."

"I'm not a man who likes to ask for favors," Mark responds. "I don't, however, dislike the idea of having them owed."

Dash laughs. "Smart man."

Mark doesn't reply. He fixes me in a steely look. "You're not coming back."

"I want to work here. I love this job and—"

"You're not coming back."

"I want to work for you in Nashville."

He studies me a long, intense moment, that turns into five, and then says, "Good thing I talked to Tyler Hawk today and made that happen. You'll handle his auctions, but all high-ticket items that are better run through the auction house directly should be looked at closely and with loyalty to us. Tyler understands this. This is a service to his clients. Anything his clients want auctioned for profit just plain comes to us. Details in your email, but be prepared for an expectation that you work for us, not him."

I blink, not completely surprised, but still surprised that this all came together this easily. "Thank you. This is exactly what I'd hoped for."

He stands and we follow him to his feet. "Then I suggest you get on a plane and make this last-minute mess of an auction Tyler Hawk has placed on our heads go over in a manner worthy of Riptide."

"I don't know how to thank you."

"You already did," he surprises me by saying. "My mother has been talking to your mother and it's helped."

This twists me in a few knots. Queen Compton is a powerful, strong, beautiful woman, weakened by the same illness that tried to break my equally powerful, strong, beautiful mother.

As if Mark reads my mind, he says, "Yes, going home is a good thing, Ms. Wright."

I'm reminded then that Mark lived in San Francisco when his mom became ill. He too went *home.*

"Can I see her before I leave?"

"Her immune system is low. She's not feeling well today, but call her tomorrow."

"I will," I say. "I absolutely will."

Dash and Mark shake hands and I have this moment where I'm taken aback by how good-looking and intensely male both of these men are, and yet, how different. Mark is absolutely the guy who bets on the fight and Dash is the guy who does the fighting. And yet, I have this sense that these two are more alike than might initially appear to be the case.

I'm also aware that these two men have worked together and helped me close this chapter of my book. I'm now opening the door to a new life and a new chapter.

It's a long time later and Dash and I have talked about Mark, Brandon, and our future over pizza, and we're now in the air, inside a private jet, snuggled into our seats. After napping a bit, I wake up to find Dash has laid his seat back and is resting. I raise my seat, dig in my briefcase and manage to pull out Allison's journal that I hadn't even realized I'd brought with me. I didn't, did I? I mean, I guess I did.

I open to a page and start reading:

In life, there are forks in the road. You choose left, and it could be right. You choose right, and it could be wrong. I know I write the same thing over and over, but that's what's happening in my head. I'm on replay and the only one I have to talk to is myself.

When I first met him, he was left, and left was right. I'd lost everyone in my life. My mom—God, I miss her, she was all I had left. My father the year I graduated college. My sister when I was still in college. She and I had been like the two musketeers. If you count her cat Molly, then well, the three musketeers. I loved that cat too and even she is gone. But back to him, *because let's just face it, he still consumes me. It's as if I was a lonely star in a pitch-dark night sky, so very alone, and this light appeared beside me. He appeared in my life.*

At first, I thought it was the sex.

The sex was intense. The way he touched me, the way he demanded more, and more, and more, and somehow, I set aside every fear and inhibition and gave him everything and more. I felt safe with him, safe in finding a new side of me, a new part of me. How many people can any of us say in life did that for us?

I glance over at Dash and suck in a breath, emotions tightening in my chest. He makes me feel all those things, all the same things Allison felt for whoever this man was she was dating. *Tyler,* I think, of course. Dash told me she was seeing Tyler.

I glance back at the page and continue reading:

I loved him. I believe he loved me, too. I still love him and yet, we are no more. I saw a part of him that was real, flawed, human, and he didn't just push me away, he pushed me far away and shoved the door shut. And now that sky is darker than ever and I'm nothing but a fallen star. I have to let him go. I have to just let go. But it hurts. And I don't know what to do. I've tried to date. I've prayed for someone who will carry me away, even just drown me in sex, please God, let me feel something other than pain.

Fear jabs at me, fear she might have hurt herself, and I quickly turn the page.

The next page reads:

I'm alive again. I met someone new. He's not him, but there are similarities. He's an older, more mature version of the one I loved. Maybe that doesn't mean love again, but I'm lost in the moment. It feels wrong for reasons I can't make myself write down. In fact, I'm not sure I'll write about this at all. Maybe that means it absolutely is wrong. Or maybe it means it's right enough that I can just live in the moment and not write it all down. We'll see...

I shut the journal and slide it into my bag. She was starting over. The way I'm starting over. For me, it feels right. But that's not what Allison said. She said something about her new relationship felt wrong. And now she's gone. I'm going to find her. And I'm going to continue finding myself.

In Nashville...

PART TWO: NASHVILLE

LISA RENEE JONES

CHAPTER TWENTY-FIVE

There are moments in life that feel eternal. Some are painful. Some are blissful. Some are just plain surreal. The moment I walk back into the Nashville apartment and it feels like home, is one of those surreal moments. Waking up Monday morning next to Dash in *our bed* is another surreal moment. Sitting at *our* kitchen island, him shirtless because I'm in his shirt, drinking coffee, and reading Dash's headline story on any number of news sites, is more a time of relief.

Brandon cannot use Dash's fighting against him. Dash took his power from him, or anyone else. Dash's cellphone rings for about the tenth time, and as he has every time before, he eyes the caller ID, and declines the call. "More reporters," he says. "More film people."

"Should you talk to the film people?"

His eyes twinkle with mischief. "I'll play hard to get with everyone but you, baby."

"You play that game well, including with me, back in New York, at that fight club."

"I followed you the minute you walked out of my room," he argues.

"And let me go."

"Only long enough to pull out of the fight I should never have been in to start with. *You* whipped my ass and I deserved it." He motions to the story on my computer screen and says, "And now I can't go back. It's no longer a secret." He angles his chair toward me and twists me around to face him, his hands on my upper thighs. "One of the reasons I did that story was to make sure you knew I'm done with that. I'm with you. At our home. I will never pull that bullshit again."

"It *was* bullshit, Dash Black."

His lips curve. "So long as you tell it how it is, baby."

I laugh. "You know I will."

"Good. Since I became a public figure, most people blow smoke up my ass. I don't like it. You and Bella keep things real and keep me grounded."

"Maybe a little smoke is a good thing considering how exceptional you are at self-hate." I press my hand to his face. "We're going to work on that. Maybe one day you'll love you as much as I do."

He captures my hand, his energy sudden sharper, darker. "Or maybe one day you'll learn to hate me, too, Allie."

In other words, the things he didn't tell me about the night his brother died are the parts that hurt the most. They're also the parts he feels I can't handle, because he can't handle them, But I don't tell him any of these things, I don't push him to tell what he's not ready to tell. I simply say, "Never."

My cellphone rings where it rests on the counter, and when I would ignore it, Dash glances at the caller ID and says, "Your mother. I'm guessing she read my interview." He kisses my hand. "Talk to her, cupcake." He stands and walks to the coffee pot, filling his cup and warming mine.

I answer the line with, "Morning, Mother."

"Oh my God. I read the interview with Dash." I glance at Dash and nod, letting him know he nailed it on the reason for her call. "He practically said he wanted to marry you."

I'd expected her to worry about his fighting, but no, she went straight to a place I haven't dared. And now there are butterflies in my belly. "No," I say. "He did not." And when I feel Dash's eyes on me, I quickly try to frame the conversation. "He tried to keep it all hush-

hush, but he gets too much attention not to have rumors start he didn't need right now."

"You're ignoring the marriage thing."

"That plot point doesn't spoil anything," I say talking about the book, and where the fighting comes into play, rather than a wedding ring.

"He's right there," she assumes. "Of course, he's right there, you live with him. He loves you."

"That's true," I confirm.

"And you love him."

"Yes, Mom," I say, and then change the topic, moving away from the awkwardness of this conversation being had in front of Dash. "You spoke with Mrs. Compton?"

"You mean Dana," she says. "Yes. She's a lovely person. And I understand everything she feels. I'm so thankful you connected us. I think we're going to be friends for life and we've only just met each other."

"How is she?"

"She's weathering the storm. Right now, her doctors are happy with her progress, but her case was worse than mine. I'm praying our lifetime of friendship is a long one. I'm hopeful that it will be."

My mother and Queen Compton come from two different worlds, one from money and power, while my mother has lived a humble life, and yet, I see them both as nurturing in their own ways. "I pray so, too, Mom. She's been really inspiring to me. She was also there at a bad time in my life."

"When you broke up with Brandon."

"Yes." Guilt stabs at me. "Mom, I never told you—"

"That he was your father's agent?"

My eyes go wide. "You knew?"

"Of course, I knew. Your father couldn't wait to call and gloat about you being there in New York with him."

"Mom—"

"It's okay, honey. I knew you'd want to know him at some point. I didn't keep him away from you. And I'm sorry he disappointed you."

"How did you know that?"

"Because I know him. No other way. I promise."

"I'll tell you the story, but not over the holiday."

"No. Not over the holiday. Let's embrace our new family with Dash and Bella. And if you don't get a ring for Christmas, I'll be as shocked as I would have been if your father was a changed man. Love you, honey. Come to Sunday brunch soon." She groans before I can answer and says, "Your stepfather is calling me. He lost his glasses. They're probably on his head."

We laugh and say our goodbyes.

Dash sits back down beside me and sips from his cup as I do the same. "That sounded like an interesting conversation."

"She knew I'd connected with my father."

"How?"

I set my cup down and rotate to face him more fully. "He told her. God, I feel bad, Dash. Like I betrayed her."

"From what I know of your mother, I think she's pretty forgiving. When did your father call her?"

"Back when I first connected with him. I had no idea."

"And *was* she angry?"

"No. She said she expected me to connect with him at some point in my life. But that doesn't mean she wasn't hurt when it was happening."

"There's an old saying. If you love someone, set them free. If they don't come back, they were never yours. That's not exact, but you get the idea. You came back to her. She knows you love her."

"Like you came back to me?" I dare to challenge.

His hands settle on my legs. "You are the calm in the storm that no one else but you knows is my life. And I'm sorry if I made you feel anything but how important you are to me, Allie. I was lost in the emotions my father made me feel. I didn't want you to get trapped in a storm of my creation."

"But you agree now that we have to ride out the storms together, right?"

"Yes," he confirms. "Together."

The doorbell rings, and Dash groans. "That's going to be Bella." He pushes to his feet, effectively ending our conversation.

Considering I'm barely dressed, I say, "I'll go shower."

He lifts me and helps me off the stool, before he says, once again. "Together, Allie."

The doorbell rings again and he growls under his breath. "My damn sister." He heads for the door and I hurry upstairs.

A few minutes later, I'm under the stream of the shower and I'm replaying Dash's vow of *together* to me. The problem is he also told me I might end up hating him. Until he dares to tell me everything, to bare his soul, we are vulnerable. And that's about trust. He doesn't trust me to love him in the good, bad, and the ugly. No. He's not going to ask me to marry him. And even if he did, I couldn't say yes, not yet. Not until I know we don't just weather the next storm together. We survive it.

And there will be another storm.

CHAPTER TWENTY-SIX

Turns out our visitor was not Bella, which I discover when Dash joins me in the shower. I don't have a lot of time to ask who the heck was at our door so early either, because his mouth is on my mouth and his hands are all over my naked body. And he's naked. Of course, he's naked, we're in the shower. And how can I think of anything when he's naked? A storm is coming all right, and at least for now, it's a good kind, right here under the spray of water, in our very own bathroom. I lose myself in the moment, in Dash, in *being home* with him, and everything good that makes me feel.

Not such a long time later, after dressing in one of my favorite black skirts, a black blazer, and a pale peachy blouse, I find a huge box on the kitchen counter.

"From my publisher," Dash says, joining me at the counter, now dressed in black jeans and a matching T-shirt. "A congratulations for the great press."

"They really do kiss your ass, don't they?"

He laughs. "Yes, well, one poor-selling book and they'll forget my name."

"That's true," I say. "I didn't like that about publishing." I tap the top of the box. "What is it?"

"A shit ton of pastries and tickets to the next Keith Urban concert here in Nashville."

Now he has my attention. I abandon the idea of a pastry for breakfast, focused on what matters. "You're kidding me. When?"

"Two weeks. Fifth row. There are four tickets. I figured we could take your mom and stepdad if you think they'll like it?"

"My God, yes, Dash. They'll be elated but what about Bella?"

"It's the weekend before Thanksgiving. Thanks to NASCAR testing an extended season this year, she's going to see her dad race."

I wrap my arms around him, tilting my chin up to meet his gaze. "Thank you for thinking of my family."

His hand flattens on my lower back, molding me closer. "I'd like to think of them as my family, too, baby." His voice is low, silky.

My mother's marriage comment is back in my head. I can't help it. He put it there with that comment. "They are," I assure him. "You know they are."

"I'm starting to feel that and it's good, Allie."

"Well, as family, I must inform you that you're officially on tree duty."

He laughs and releases me, reaching for his coffee cup. "What does tree duty entail?"

"It means you get to put up not one, but two trees."

He arches a brow. "Two?"

"My parent's tree and ours, I hope." I reclaim my barstool. "It's kind of a family tradition to put it up on Thanksgiving. What do you normally do?"

"Since my mother died, nothing. Bella does it all. She bitches I don't have a tree and rushes in here and puts one up. I have one in the storage room downstairs. There's a bunch of the decorations we had with my mother as well."

"Bella is an angel. And I can't wait to see it. Is Thanksgiving night okay?"

"I think for the first time in a long time, the answer is yes."

"Should we invite Bella over? Actually," I say, as a thought hits me. "What if we host a tree trimming party and I invite my mom and stepdad? My mom is dying to see what the apartment is like."

"When?"

"How about the Saturday after Thanksgiving? It can be a new tradition."

His eyes and his voice warm. "I like that, Allie. Very much."

Now, I warm. "Perfect."

"Yes. Yes, it is," he agrees. "Trust the magic of new beginnings, baby. And yes, that is a quote, and no, I don't know who said it. I read it. Somewhere. Probably on the internet, about the time I left the FBI behind. And here I am. And here you are. Where you belong, Allie."

"Yes," I say softly. "Here I am. Where I belong."

And for the first time, I dare to believe this is where I will stay.

To hell with the storm.

LISA RENEE JONES

CHAPTER TWENTY-SEVEN

Turns out, the pastries are really good pastries. I eat one and wrap one up to take with me on the road. "I really want to get to work early."

"I'll go with you," Dash suggests, finishing off a pastry of his own. "I need to write and I do that better at certain stages of the book when I'm not at home and easily distracted. I'll head over to Cupcakes and Books."

I glance at my watch. "Are they open?"

"I have a key. Jackson and Adrianna let me go in through the employee entrance and start working before the doors open."

"That's a sweet deal, quite literally," I joke.

"That's right, cupcake," he says with a wink, and then we bundle up and he walks me to Hawk Legal, where we make plans for lunch.

Dash and I part ways with a kiss and a shared smile that carries me inside the building, leaving him behind, but not for long. I'm feeling that whole surreal sensation again. I'd been so alone when I met Dash and I'd almost convinced myself that's what I wanted. Now, I can't imagine life without him and that's the scary thing. While I know he's committed and so am I, I can't shake the certainty that there is that storm cloud hovering, and sooner or later, it will burst. I shove aside that thought and focus on the task ahead of me.

Mark has told me I have a job. Tyler has not. This is a two-way street. While yes, I could work from home, and still manage the annual charity and year-round auctions, I'm not sure how that would really work out. Bottom line, I'm celebrating a future that requires three signatures and I only have two. Mine and Mark's. I need

Tyler's, which is exactly why when I step off the elevator I head straight to my office, or what I hope is my office, dump my things and then make my way to his office. It's early, but Tyler tends to be in the office before everyone and he often stays until the place is dark. I'm not sure if that means he's devoted to his work, or hiding from his personal life. Maybe both. I understand both. That was my story before I met Dash.

As expected, his secretary is not in yet, but a peak down the hallway tells me the light to his office is shining brightly.

I hurry in that direction and step into his doorway. Tyler is standing in front of the window, as I found him once before, staring out at the city. I wonder what a man like Tyler contemplates so intensely. The words I'd read in the journal last night come back to me:

I loved him. I believe he loved me, too. I still love him and yet, we are no more.

I wonder if Allison is on his mind.

I wonder if she's moved on and is happy.

I wonder why I can't believe that to be true.

Tyler turns to face me. "You don't work for me anymore, Ms. Wright, and yet, I get the feeling you still aspire to continue to be the first and last person to harass me today."

"Harass you?" I challenge, a bit amused at this remark. "Is that what I'm doing?"

"I haven't had coffee this morning. So, yes. You're harassing me, as would anyone else who spoke to me right now."

"Should I go get you a coffee and come back?"

"The part where you come back doesn't work for me."

"Okay then. You're obviously pissed at me, right?"

"No," he replies flatly. "I am not *pissed at you,* though a warning about Mark Compton calling me would have been appreciated."

"I didn't know. I didn't even plan to be back here today, because of—"

"Dash. I know. I told you he's fucked up. You didn't listen."

"Aren't we all, Tyler?"

"I believe we're repeating a previous argument. No coffee, Ms. Wright. Remember?"

"This keeps going sideways. Deny what you will, but we both know you're really angry at me."

He scrubs his jaw in an act of frustration, not his normal cool confidence and control, then settles his hands on his hips under his jacket before he motions to the door. "Let's go have coffee, Allie. Not here."

I blink in surprise both at the use of my first name and at his invitation. Or whatever it is. "I need to get my coat."

"I'll meet you at the elevator."

I nod and turn away, walking toward the door.

No one else is here, but he wants out of the building, where we can talk.

I'm not sure what's going on, but it doesn't feel like it's anything good.

CHAPTER TWENTY-EIGHT

I'm about to exit his office when Tyler says, "Wait."

I rotate to face him again, my nerves crackling and popping at his weird behavior, not sure what to expect next. "I have a damn meeting," he says. "I put on a pot of coffee. In the break room."

Confused by him being so indecisive, I just go with the flow. "Okay. I'll get the coffee. How do you like it?"

"You're not my damn servant, Allie." He closes the space between us and motions me to the hallway. "I need coffee."

I don't know what is going on with him right now, but I don't push him. I turn and exit and start walking, with him behind me instead of beside me. Talk about awkward. I cut into the break room and quickly dart for the mugs sitting beside the pot. I set two on the counter and fill them both. Tyler steps close beside me, really close, and I smell him—spicy and male—but different from Dash. I don't even feel comfortable knowing how he smells.

Tyler and I have a connection. I know this. I'm drawn to him, but it has nothing to do with me wanting him. I think it's about being alone. Because I was alone when I met him. Because he's still alone. And I fear being alone again. On some level, even as I have this thought, I recognize this as a flaw. I was okay alone. I shouldn't fear being in that place again. I don't fear it, I amend.

I fear being without Dash.

Somehow I've had this entire internal conversation with myself and still managed to pour cream and Splenda into my coffee. Tyler has done the same. He glances over at me, his steely eyes meeting mine, and for a few seconds, we just stare at each other. I'm not sure what he's looking for and I can't read him. The longer this continues, the more uneasy I feel.

"Tyler?" I ask, uncertainty in my tone, I don't try to hide.

"My office," he says, picking up his cup and starting in that direction.

He exits the break room and I follow. Now I'm behind him and somehow this is just as awkward as the opposite. He enters his office and angles toward me long enough to motion me to the conference table. "Sit."

It's an impatient command. I do as he says because 1) I filled my cup too full and it's going to spill if I get fired up one little bit and Tyler is pretty good at getting me fired up, and 2) I want to know what's going on. I settle into my seat and Tyler sits across from me, sipping his coffee. I do the same. It's good coffee, cinnamon, I think. Figures he'd favor good coffee. He works all the time, so fueling up is a necessity.

"You saw the interview?" I ask when he just looks at me again.

"I approved it before Bella made it happen."

"Then you're pleased." It's not really a question, and yet, it's kind of a question. He's just too weird to make assumptions with at present.

"For now," he states. "When I told you he's fucked up, I wasn't speaking out of malice. I was speaking a fact. He'll screw up again. And he managed to draw you back in to hurt you all over again."

My defenses flare, my need to protect Dash right along with them. "You don't know what happened between me and Dash."

"You're going to tell me he didn't hurt you this weekend?"

"Do I have a job, Tyler?" I snap back, the snap hard to avoid.

"You work for Riptide. They're renting your office for a sizable premium."

"Then can I go?"

"No," he states. "You cannot. You still work for me, even if it is as a contractor." He softens his voice. "He will hurt you, Allie. You need to wake up."

"You don't know—"

"Why do you think he got so mad in that club when I said he was no good for you?"

"Because it was a lousy thing to say in front of me?"

"Because when he said it to me about another woman, I listened. I stepped back. I made the decision to think about her, not me. He should do the same. He will not."

My lips purse. "This isn't about me and Dash. It's about you and Allison."

"In or out, because if you're not in all the way, you need to walk away now before this gets dirty and bad for both of you."

"Is this personal or professional?"

"In or out," he repeats. "No matter how dirty it gets."

I blanch and do a double-take. "You know why his father hates him."

"Do you?" he challenges.

"I'm asking if you do."

His eyes sharpen. "In other words, you don't know, at least not everything." He picks up his coffee. "Let's talk about the auction."

"She loved you."

"I know," he says, his voice without emotion, but his eyes burn with a hint of anger and I'm not sure that anger is directed at me.

"You loved her," I dare.

LISA RENEE JONES

"The auction."

I draw in a breath and fight anger at his implication that Dash is selfish to stay with me. I want to tell him that he's selfish for the words he's saying to me, but I'm not sure that's where this comes from. I'm not sure of a lot of things and won't be until I have time to think. Alone. So I tell him about the auction. When I'm done, he says, "It's sound like you've done an exceptional job for us, Riptide, and the cause."

"Does that mean you want me to stay on?"

"I want a lot of things with you, Allie."

There is a pop of tension between us that feels sexual, and I'd accuse him of trying to hurt Dash, but there's more to this. I feel it. I sense it. "Because I remind you of her."

He just looks at me—he's doing way too much of that—before he says, "I want you to work for Hawk Legal, not Riptide. I'll give you a twenty percent raise and a twenty-thousand-dollar signing bonus."

"Why would you do that? You have me for free."

"You don't need the money when you're with Dash, but then, you don't need the money anyway. If Dash's money motivated you, so would your father's."

"Okay," I say cautiously. "If you know that, then again, why, Tyler?"

"Because the minute something goes wrong with Dash, you're back in New York, and I'm starting over. You don't get to have one foot in the door and one foot out. If you want to be here, be here. For me and for *him.*"

"My job doesn't change if something happens between me and Dash. I like what I'm doing. I want to be here."

"Good. Then I'll have human resources draw up the paperwork."

"No."

He arches a brow. "No?"

"I promised Mark loyalty."

"And what do you promise me?"

"Loyalty in this partnership. I'm not going to leave. And why would you tell Mark this was okay if it wasn't?"

"I told Mark the opportunity to work with Riptide makes sense for us. I didn't agree to the terms he presented. You have my terms. Mark and I agreed you'd finish this year on my payroll. You have until December thirty-first to make your decision."

He stands up. I do the same. "Tyler—"

"My offer stands."

"And what do I tell Mark?"

"I plan to call and tell him myself."

"If you tell him now, he'll force my decision immediately. Don't do that to me."

"Now would be better than later."

"And you could end up with an auction that flounders, fails, or doesn't happen."

"December thirty-first," he says tightly.

"I don't understand why you're doing this."

"You should. Maybe if you think a little harder, you will."

I don't know what is happening here, but it's clearly not exactly what I think. I draw in a breath and turn and walk toward the door, but then I turn and face him. "She didn't leave you. You sent her away. You weren't willing to be vulnerable with her."

"And Dash is with you?"

"Yes."

"You sure about that? Because if you'd made your decision about him, really made it, you wouldn't leave an open door. Think about it."

He's wrong, but there's no explaining myself to him and I'm not sure I can try. There's more to this meeting

139

than meets the eye. "She didn't leave you," I repeat. "You left her while you were still standing right in front of her. Call her. I know you love her."

"I have called her, Allie." His voice vibrates. "She won't call me back."

I hurry back toward him. "I'm worried about her. Aren't you worried?"

"She hates me, Allie."

"There's a fine line between love and hate. Nothing about her leaving and ghosting everyone makes sense. I'm worried. Worry with me and let's find her."

"And then what?"

"Then you get on your damn knees and you beg her to forgive you. Think about it. You may not have until December thirty-first. Maybe she doesn't, either." I whirl on my heel and march for the door, hoping he'll stop me. He doesn't.

CHAPTER TWENTY-NINE

I walk into my office, or at least, the office I'm using, and shut the door before I sit down. My first instinct is to call Dash. I dig my phone from my pocket, but I pause with a second thought. Dash already knows Tyler was involved with all that happened this weekend. I have to tell him about this, but doing it when I'm fired up and emotional isn't the best idea. I'll talk to him over lunch. I set my phone aside and my mind is on Allison. How can it not be? Everything that just happened has something to do with her. That was fairly obvious, at least to me.

I grab my phone again and punch in Allison's number. It goes straight to voicemail and this time when it answers, I say, "Allison. My name is also Allison. But I'm not calling about filling in for you at Hawk Legal. I'm calling about Tyler. He's miserable without you. That's easy to see. He's burning alive in the flames of his own regret." I laugh awkwardly. "That sounded intense. I used to be an editor. Can you tell? Please come back. Or call him. There's nothing between me and him. I'm happily with someone else. There were just circumstances and I—well, I found your journal, and please forgive me, but I started reading—and I'm—I feel like I know you. It's silly, but it's like we're friends. Maybe we really can be and—

The machine beeps.

I call back and this time when the machine answers I say, "Come back, Allison. Or call. If not him, me. Just let us know you're okay. *Please.*"

I disconnect.

I'm a stranger. That message probably means nothing to her, but I had to try.

I open my drawer and stare down at my purse, where the journal remains, and I can't help myself. I reach for it, hoping for an answer to a question I'm not even aware I should be asking. If I found her, it just feels as if the world would be right. Tyler would be a new man. A man I've never met and perhaps no one has. Unable to help myself, I pick up the journal, praying for something that helps me find Allison, or just to know she's safe. I open to the final page. It's blank. So are the ten pages before it and the ten before those. I find the final entry and start reading:

In times like these, I miss my mother more than ever. I also realize my friendships here in Nashville are all plastic. There is no one I feel comfortable telling my secrets to. Let's face it, that's why I started writing a journal. I have no one. Maybe that's why I fell so hard for him. And I did. So ridiculously hard. I want to go to him, but he'd never forgive me. All I would do is put a nail in our coffin, but then, what choice do I have? He has to know. And yet, it will hurt him. He hurt me, but I have no wish to hurt him.

I don't know what to do.

Everything in my life is spinning out of control. Everything has gone so very wrong. I feel as if it's my fault when I know it wasn't my fault at all. It's victim-blaming, right? The victim does it and then the rest of the world has an invitation to do it as well. But then, I haven't told anyone what happened for me to be blamed. The truth is that I feel guilt. I went down a path I should have never traveled. I was wrong. I was a bad person and I deserve everything that brings me. But if I confess, I hurt him and probably many others. If I don't tell, someone else is certainly going to be hurt.

Like I was hurt. Someone else will end up like me. I'm sure there has been someone before me, someone who suffered in silence and let this happen to me. I feel so damn angry with whoever that was. I don't want someone else to feel that about me. I don't know what to do and if only these pages could answer me and tell me what to do.

God, I have to tell him. I have to go to him. It's the right move. Isn't it? I want to throw this book against the wall, but then I'll be even more alone. Maybe I'll call him now. Maybe I'll just sit on this and think. How did I end up here? I wish I could go back to the times I spent with him, asleep with him, awake with him, naked with him. I should have never told him I loved him. I should have never let him know I saw everything. He wasn't ready for me to see everything.

That's it. Nothing more.

I flip several pages back, looking for entries that tell me what this means, but nothing in the recent pages read with this tone at all. In fact, they're about the auction. I skim and it's clear she was excited about the event. I go back to the final entry, a chill running down my spine as I read: *He wasn't ready for me to see everything.*

Just like Dash.

I swear so many times Allison's words have spoken to me. In this case, it's a reminder to not let Tyler's words get to me. Tyler keeps pushing every button there is to push with me and Dash, and more and more I feel like it's really about him and Allison, not me and Dash.

CHAPTER THIRTY

My attention returns to the journal and Allison. I read the entry I've just read again and decide that it's possible she ran from her problems. I let that simmer a moment, but reject this possibility and do so out of logic, not emotion. I don't feel it's likely that she'd leave the man she loved without talking to him. Of course, that theory assumes she didn't talk to Tyler. Maybe she did and he shut her out. I scan the passage again and turn to two sentences: *If I don't tell, someone else is certainly going to be hurt. Like I was hurt.*

Unease burns in my belly with the words, *like I was hurt.*

I grab my phone and dial Dash. He answers on the first ring. "Miss me already?"

"No, I mean yes, of course, but—it's been a weird morning."

"Already?"

"I had a conversation with Tyler that kind of ties into why I called." I don't give him time to ask questions or comment adding, "I still have that journal I found. And before you say anything, the talk with Tyler just triggered my worries about Allison again therefore I grabbed it from my purse—"

"You're carrying it around?"

"Yes, well, I guess I am. The point is the final entry— it's—I don't know what it is. I'm going to take a photo and send it to you and just let you read it. Hold on a minute." I shoot the photo and text it to Dash. "You should get it any second."

"I got it. Give me a minute to read." He's silent for a good thirty seconds before he says, "I'm not sure if this makes me feel like she ran or got herself in trouble by talking to the wrong person."

"I know, right? I felt the same. Should I talk to Tyler about it and ask what he knows?"

"He'll want to see the journal. Are you prepared to show it to him?"

"It's bad enough that I'm reading it and showing part of it to you. No. Not now. I don't think so. There has to be another way for me to bring it up. I could say I heard a rumor, maybe?"

"Maybe," he says, "but before you do anything we need to pause. Neil texted me this morning anyway. He wants us to meet at lunch. Can you still make that happen?"

"Yes, I'll make it happen. Does he have news?"

"He wants to update us on what he's discovered, but he was matter-of-fact about it."

"How very FBI agent of him. Does he have news?" I repeat.

"I'd tell you if I knew, baby, but bring the journal."

"I don't want Neil to have it," I say, appalled at the idea.

"I get that, but if we had chosen to file a missing person's report, they'd want it. Better Neil than an entire police department."

"I need this journal, Dash," I say, the word "need" clawing at me. "I feel a bit like I'm her only advocate and maybe one of the only people who could understand some of what is inside."

He's silent a moment, disapproval ticking through the line before he says, "Make copies if you can. If not, I'll have him make them and bring the journal back."

"Tell me I'm worrying for nothing."

"I'll wait until after I hear what Neil has to say. *You* tell *me* what happened with Tyler."

"Only if you promise me you'll let me handle Tyler."

"That depends," he says, his voice hard as stone. "Did he put his hands on you or hit on you?"

"No." I hesitate, thinking about that one moment with Tyler when he'd said, *"there's a lot of things I want to do with you."*

"Not really," I add.

"Not really?" Dash snaps. "What the hell, Allie?"

"He didn't. It's not that simple. He told me I had to be in or out with you because you'll fuck up again and basically, paraphrasing, of course, I don't get to cut and run from my job, if we break-up. Again, not exactly what he said, but that was how I read his message. It's very confusing because why does he care? I mean, in one breath he warns me away from you, and in the next, he's telling me to commit. I think. He's very confusing."

"What else?" he asks tightly.

"He told me I can only work for Hawk directly. He won't let me have one foot in the door and one out with Riptide and New York versus Hawk Legal and Nashville."

He's silent two beats before he asks, "And you said what to all of this?" his tone unreadable, cautiously controlled, no doubt.

"Not much. As little as possible. We are *not* his business and besides that conversation wasn't about me or you. It was about him and Allison, and on that, I did speak. I told him I knew that. I told him to call her. He told me she hates him. Maybe she went to him about whatever happened and he reacted poorly and she just had enough. She left. You have no idea how much I want to believe that or how much I can't seem to actually believe it. I don't why this is nagging at me. But since I found the journal, hearing her words in my head, knowing how alone she is, just really makes me feel like she needs us."

"Which I understand. But if you're right and she got into trouble, my problem with all of this is that you're in the middle."

"I'm really not."

"Unless you are. We have no idea what she was talking about, but I don't like how it sounds. *Someone else will get hurt, like I got hurt.* Those words, Allie. I do not want that someone else to be you."

"Which is why I need to figure out how to talk to Tyler. On that note, are you going to comment about what Tyler said about you or us?"

"What did it mean to you, Allie?"

"He doesn't know who we are together, Dash. I do."

"What did you say to him about us? Don't tell me you said nothing."

"All I said was that I'm all in. I'm not going anywhere."

He's silent a moment and then he says, "I'll see you at lunch, cupcake."

"Okay. Yes. But for the record, I know you're bothered by all of this and I want to talk about it. But you need to go write and I have to work."

"Yes," he says. "We need to talk. And yes, to all the rest, too."

"I love you, Dash."

"I love you, too, Allie. More than you know."

He disconnects.

He is not pleased. Tyler is not pleased. And I have this sensation of being inside a bubbling pot about to boil over.

CHAPTER THIRTY-ONE

The minute Katie realizes I'm back at work, she's at my side and drilling me with questions about the auction. Everyone seems to find me shortly after she does, from Millie Roberts at the charity organization, to clients participating in the auction with various inquiries. This makes copying the journal in private a challenge. Thankfully, I remember that the upstairs rooftop where the event is to be held not only has a copy machine in one corner, it's also closed for use to the employees. With this in mind, just before lunch, I tell everyone I'm leaving and instead head there, purse on my shoulder, journal in my purse.

Once I'm inside the rooftop area, I give it a once over and decide it really is going to be a perfect spot for the auction and thankfully, I got notice today that the hotel refunded us completely. Now invitations can be printed and delivered, which needs to happen pretty much now. With all this and more bouncing around in my head, I rush to the copy machine, plop my purse on the table next to it, and pull out the journal. I'm deep into the process, almost done, in fact, when I hear, "You must be the new Allison."

I jump with the unfamiliar male voice and look up to find a tall, good-looking man with sandy brown hair and striking green eyes standing beside me. "Sorry," he says. "I didn't mean to scare you."

"I—ah, who are you? No one is allowed in here."

"You're here," he says, as I turn to face him and him me.

"Yes, but being here is a part of my job."

"I work here as well," he assures me.

I'm aware of how tall and broad he is, how well-fitted his suit is, which could indicate he's a principal in the company, or not. I don't know. Which is why I don't scold him again. "I am, in fact, Allison," I say, prodding him for an introduction, which he offers.

"I'm Benjamin. Benji to my friends, which I'd like to call you." He laughs. "I hated that nickname in my youth, but I guess in time all things can grow on you."

He's mid-thirties, I believe, perhaps older, and I do know the name. I just don't know why.

"I had a few of my clients donate to the auction," he states, as if he's reading my mind, and that's when I realize he's one of the agents.

"Right," I say, remembering an email or two exchanged with him. "I remember. Thank you for doing that."

"My pleasure. I'll help any way I can." He glances at the copy machine. "Looks like Allison left you some notes."

I quickly grab the papers and straighten them, just to look like I'm working, not hiding the words on the page. "Lists and lists of contacts as potential donors. Katie is going to split them up with me."

"I always thought that journal of hers was personal. But knowing Allison, it makes sense it was work. She was nothing if not devoted to this place."

"You knew her well?"

"We knew each other and I know this is a big job and you've been thrown into this. I can have my secretary help."

"No, but thank you," I say surprised by the generous offer, but also a bit suspicious. "We're a good team, me and Katie. Tyler assigned her to help me full-time for now. We can get it all done."

"Tyler," he states, a quirk to his lips. "You actually call him Tyler? No one else is allowed to. What'd you do to earn that honor?"

I laugh nervously. "Not to his face, I don't. It's confusing to say Mr. Hawk to anyone who isn't him when his father is also Mr. Hawk."

"His father favors his first name. Those two are nothing alike."

"Is that good or bad?"

"I'll keep those opinions to myself," he replies dryly. "What do you think?"

"I'm too new to have an opinion."

"Good out," he teases and he doesn't seem to have any intention of leaving. "Funny how your name is Allison."

"Allie," I say. "I go by Allie."

"Allie," he says. "Are you staying with Hawk Legal?'

"I haven't decided."

"Can I take you to lunch? Maybe you can fill me in a bit more on your needs and I can be of service."

There is something highly suggestive in his tone and the way he's looking at me. "I'm having lunch with Dash Black."

"Oh right. This is his charity. I don't know him. What's he like? An arrogant prick? Most of our clients are."

"Well, I actually live with him, so, no. I don't believe he's an arrogant prick."

"Well, open mouth and insert foot. Good thing I didn't actually call him a prick. And actually, isn't he related to Bella?"

"Half-sister," I say. "Fortunately, she doesn't think he's an arrogant prick either."

"I heard he had some big PR piece today. I'm a little more interested now. I think I'll read it. The lunch offer is open." He starts to step away and then says, "You look so much like her. I wasn't surprised she left, but then, you two are so alike, it's as if she was still here." He walks away and I turn to watch him leave.

Why does the way he said *"it's as if she's still here"* send a chill down my spine? I hug myself, bothered by everything about this encounter. And he knew she kept a journal? I'm creeped out.

CHAPTER THIRTY-TWO

When I arrive at the bookstore, Dash and Neil are already at a table talking. At least, I assume the man with him is Neil. I've never actually met him. Adrianna is behind the counter and I wave to her. "You want your usual?" she calls out.

"Yes, please," I say, which translates to a ham and cheese croissant and a diet soda, therefore justifying the cupcake that will follow. Everyone knows if you drink a diet soda, a cupcake is allowed. It's logical.

I arrive at the table and Dash and Neil both stand up. Neil is about Dash's age, and also like Dash, is wearing jeans and a T-shirt. He's tall, muscular, but lean, and his hair is buzzed, almost as if he just got out of the Army, which I assume means he's ex-Army. He shakes my hand and says, "You follow orders horribly."

"So says my mother right before I remind her I'm an adult."

The two men laugh, deep rumbles of masculine laughter, and Neil says, "Point taken."

Dash kisses me, his hand on my back, especially possessive, which doesn't strike me as having anything to do with Neil. It's about Tyler. He helps me with my coat and we share a look that is all kinds of hot. It's also punched with unspoken words related to that talk I had with Tyler.

We all sit down and I look between both men, already recognizing a comfort between them. They don't just know each other. They're friends and I know for a fact Dash doesn't call many people friend. I'm fairly certain he cut people off after his brother died, but I'll have to dive a bit deeper into that later. "What do I need to know?" I ask.

"I put together an email file for both of you," Neil replies. "The most significant point I have to make is that Allison's phone last pinged here in Nashville. I've tried to locate where it's coming from, but these pings represent a general area. Which," he adds, "wouldn't concern me outside of the fact that it's no longer pinging."

All the more reason to be concerned, I think, but I try to stay hopeful. "Could that mean she got a new phone?"

"It's possible," he says, "but I don't like the way she just disappeared. And if she wanted to cut people off, she could just change her number."

"You said she was texting."

"That stopped as well," he states. "And we really can't know who was doing the texting."

"Who was she texting?"

"A friend of hers from her hometown. A couple of random people. Nothing that's worthy of note. All of which could have been done to make it look like she was okay when she was not."

"Then you're worried," I say, stating what seems to be the obvious.

"Worried enough," he confirms. "She has no living family that isn't way down the chain of connections. I talked to her friends back in her hometown and no one has heard from her."

"She's what we would call an easy victim," Dash adds. "There's no one to look for her."

My mind instantly replays the passage I read from Allison's journal and somehow the words are embedded in my memory. *In times like these, I miss my mother more than ever. I also realize my friendships here in*

Nashville are all plastic. There is no one I feel comfortable telling my secrets. Let's just face it, that's why I started writing a journal. I have no one.

"Except me," I say, knots in my belly over her emotions. "She only has me and we never even met."

"It's no different than a member of law enforcement having a missing person become personal," Neil offers. "It can become an obsession. And often it's why answers are found."

"How many times is the person found alive?" I ask.

Neil looks at Dash and Dash looks at me. "Not enough."

I appreciate the honesty, but it also twists me in knots.

"Did you bring the journal, baby?" he asks.

"Yes," I say. "I copied it." I reach into my bag and hand a folder to Neil. "Something weird," I add, looking between them. "I copied this in the rooftop event room where no one is allowed. One of the agents, Benjamin— I need to look up his last name—was just suddenly there. He recognized Allison's writing. He even said he thought her journal was for personal reasons. I told him it was her business notes. It was weird, creepy. He asked me to lunch. He offered to help me with the auction. He told me I look like her."

Dash's jaw sets hard and he eyes Neil. Neil says, "I know his last name. It's Wilson. He's on Allison's call logs and not during work hours. I'm already looking into him." He glances at me. "Stay away from him."

"Believe me, I will." I give Dash a nod and say, "I will."

He doesn't look convinced. His lips are tight as he asks Neil, "What else?"

"The last actual phone call she had was with Tyler. He's tried to call her since more than a few times. I don't believe he knows where she is. I also have a frequent caller that can't be identified. Almost as if the phone is a burner phone."

"That doesn't sound good," I say.

"No," Dash replies. "It doesn't. You're right, Allie. She's in trouble. I'd bet my book deal on it."

"So what do we do? Go to the police?"

"No," Neil replies. "They're going to make it way too obvious that you're behind this. And they aren't likely to do much without pressure. I need to find her or she may never be found. And I need to do it in a way that keeps you out of it, Allie, and off the radar of anyone that might have hurt her. I have some ideas." He sticks the file in a leather bag on the side of his chair. "I'll read the journal tonight and see if it connects any dots."

"Tyler—"

"I don't believe he hurt her. I got the code to her voicemail. His messages do not sound like a man who thinks she's dead."

Dead.

The word makes my stomach roll.

Neil slides on his jacket. "Anything else?"

I shake my head. Dash stands and says, "Keep us posted."

"I will," Neil replies and then he's walking away.

Adrianna appears with my lunch and sets it on the table. "Lunch has arrived. I didn't want to interrupt or I'd have brought it sooner. I could tell you were in deep conversation."

"Thank you," I say. "I'm starving."

She looks between us. "You look like you need me to leave. If you want coffee and a cupcake—"

"I do," I say. "To go though, please."

"You got it," she says and quickly backs away.

Dash angles toward me, his hand settling on my knee. "Can you finish the auction prep in New York? We'll get a second home there."

"Because of this Allison thing?"

"Yes. I don't appreciate Tyler's bullshit, but if we can't weather that storm, we shouldn't be together. Your safety is my concern."

"Dash, this is our home. I said my goodbyes to New York. I want to enjoy the holiday season here, with you and my mom. And Bella. And my stepfather. I don't mean to downplay him. He's family. I do love him, too."

"Your safety comes first."

"I'm fine. I'm careful. You're close. Bella is close. I'll be careful."

"Can you at least work from home halftime?"

"Yes. I can. I'll make arrangements this afternoon. I don't really think Tyler can say much at this point. He needs me to finish out the auction. He knows I'll do it because you're involved and because I care about the outcome."

"Exactly my thoughts."

"I don't know what to do about my job after this year. I really don't want to leave Riptide, but I want to be here."

"My advice. Call Mark Compton."

"I think you're right. I need to just call him. And I need to call his mom. I really love her."

"Allie. What Tyler said—"

I press my hand to his face. "Means nothing. But you do."

"I walked away from you. Family doesn't walk away from family. If I could turn back time-"

"You won't do it again. And now you know I won't let you." I manage to keep a straight face as I add, "Now you know who's in control."

He laughs, but there's anger there beneath the deep rumble. And not at me. He's angry at himself. I think that's a problem for us. He's always angry at himself. This talented, amazing man just can't let go of the past.

And as for Allison, I pray that's exactly what she did: let go of her past, and by choice.

CHAPTER THIRTY-THREE

The minute I'm in the Hawk Legal elevator headed to my floor, anger percolates in that part of my belly that cannot hold onto things. I've learned that when my emotions find that destination they're going to find a path out. Tyler is playing games with my life and I've had it to the rooftop with men who try to control me. By the time the doors open and I step out into the foyer, I turn left toward Tyler's office, not right toward the lobby and my own office.

His secretary Debbie is behind the desk and when she greets me, I say, "I'm here to see Tyler."

"I'll buzz his office."

There's no waiting for me. I storm down the hallway and when I reach his door, there's no tender footing about for me this time. I'm no newbie at interrupting Tyler and I'm still in charge mode and charge I do. I step inside his office and say, "Tyler, you need to know—" I halt and gape as I realize that he's standing behind his desk, and another man is on his feet across from him.

My heart thunders when that man turns to face me and I realize it's his father. Oh my God. I've really done it now.

"Do continue, Allie," Jack Hawk instructs, his eyes alight with what appears to be amusement. "What does *Tyler* need to know?"

Considering we've had the conversation about Tyler's formality, he's clearly pointing out my informal address of his son. "Sorry for intruding," I quickly offer. "I pulled together the list of auction items and I was excited about how fabulously the event is coming together. Which is all I wanted to say."

"Is that right?" Hawk Senior asks. His eyes are bright gray, intelligent, and calculating, and again I'm struck by how powerful an impact Hawk Senior's presence creates.

"Yes. Again, sorry for the intrusion."

"No apology needed," Hawk Senior assures me. "Good news is always welcomed with as much excitement as its delivery. And I'm glad to see you've managed to be on first name terms with my son when so few have."

"Ms. Wright tends to take liberties," Tyler replies. "She forgets herself."

Hawk Senior is another story. He laughs. "Is that right?" He gives me a tilt of his chin. "Feel free to take all the liberties you like with me. I prefer everyone here feel I'm an open book. It's Jack, in case you don't remember."

There is something about the "take all the liberties you like with me" that stirs an uneasy feeling, though I'm fairly certain that's me transferring my feelings toward Tyler onto him right now. "Of course, I remember," I assure him. "And thank you. Sometimes my excitement does get the best of me."

"Tell us more," he urges. "How do you define a successful event?"

"Yes, Ms. Wright," Tyler chimes in. "Tell us more." His tone says the last thing he wants is "more" of me right now. Or his father, I suspect, but he's a brick wall, so practiced at schooling his emotions, he has none to read.

I give them both more anyway. "At present," I say. "I believe we'll have at least three hundred thousand in final donations. There are a few prime items that could take that to five hundred thousand."

"Well then, let's shoot for seven-fifty," Jack suggests, rubbing his well-manicured hands together. "Let me call on a few of my big players."

"That's very generous of you," I say. "Thank you. I should get back to work. Sorry again for interrupting." My eyes meet Tyler's and his irritation appears to be more amusement. He's enjoying watching me squirm. Asshole.

"More from me soon, Allie," Jack promises.

"And me," Tyler adds, a smirk on his face.

I back away and give them a stupid wave. Am I really back to that wave? "Bye, thank you." I whirl around and exit the office and want to crawl under the floor—yes, the floor, that's how embarrassed I feel in this moment. But even as embarrassed as I am, somehow, I'm motivated to drive this auction to even bigger success. That's the way I operate. I like and need to please. It's both a flaw and an asset in some cases. I do believe that's how I ended up with Brandon. He pleased my father. He did not please me.

Tyler wants me to choose Hawk to please him. Part of me wants to give him what he's demanding. Even as I walk past his secretary without a word, I decide that's part of my connection to Tyler. He reminds me of the men I've tried to please in my life. In fact, I remember a psychology book I edited once and the lessons I learned. People are creatures of habit. We repeat what is familiar, and therefore safe, and that includes the bad things. A daughter of an alcoholic father often gravitates to a husband with the same issues. We repeat, to our own peril.

In that moment, I appreciate the fact that Dash didn't ask me to leave New York or my job to please him. He said he'd pick up and leave Nashville for me. And I'm not making him go to New York to please me. But I'm not going to be blackmailed by Tyler Hawk, either.

CHAPTER THIRTY-FOUR

It's midafternoon when Bella steps into my office and shuts the door. "You didn't tell me he was fighting again. I know that black eye was from a fight, too."

She looks like the business version of Cinderella in a pink silk blouse and black skirt, with her long blonde hair draped over her shoulders while I feel like the bad, ugly stepsister who did her wrong.

"I know. I'm sorry. He—"

"Didn't want to freak me out," she supplies, sitting down in the chair in front of my desk. "I know. And I get it. You didn't either."

"No, but you have no idea how much I wanted to come to you, Bella. Tyler pushed his buttons by telling Dash he wasn't good for me in front of me. It didn't end well."

"Dash told me what happened. And I know Tyler was pissed when Dash told him not to drive drunk in front of Allison. But he knows—" She stops herself. "I mean—"

"I know about the accident. His father made sure I knew and not gently."

Her lips purse. "That man knows how to hurt him, but Dash's stepmother is no better. She never liked Dash. He was competition for his father's affection and money. It was easy for her to blame Dash for her son's death. Like Dash could control him. They were in college. They were old enough to vote and enlist in the army."

"Believe me, I know. I agree. And I saw the hate firsthand."

"Dash told me you went and got him in a fight club."

"Twice," I say. "Once here and once in New York."

Her brows furrow. "Here? How did you know where to go?"

"Tyler, of course. After he confronted Dash. Dash and I had a fight, and I went home. You know where Dash went."

"To fight. Thank you, *Tyler*. God. That bastard."

"Yes, but I think he regretted pushing Dash the way he did. He knew he went too far. For all his faults, I don't think Tyler got me involved in the fight club to embarrass Dash or break us up. He just felt I could stop him from fighting. Unfortunately, I was too late that first night. Honestly, it's a godsend I found out because I knew what to expect after his dad confronted him."

"Dash told me he pushed you away and you came after him anyway. He said you were brave and stubborn and that he doesn't deserve you but he can't let you go. Allie, he loves you or he would never have named you in that article today. He also wouldn't have outed himself. He could have found another way to beat Brandon. By doing this the way he did it, he made sure he can't go fight again, he can't hide in that world."

"And I love him," I say softly, emotion welling in my throat. "I love him very much."

She squeezes my hand. "Thank you for taking care of my brother." She releases my hand and smiles. "And for the invite to Thanksgiving. I can't wait."

"I'm so glad you're coming. And I want to hear all about your father."

She stands up and rounds the desk. I'm on my feet when she gets to me and we hug before she looks at me. "I have a feeling we're going to get to know each other very well, Allie. And now, I have to get back to work." She heads to the door and pauses, "I have one of my most arrogant, pompous clients in contract negotiations. He's nice to me, but good grief, I have to reel him in with that mouth of his or he'll shoot himself in the foot and his wallet."

I laugh and she exits the office. I decide the universe just sent me another sign that this is home.

Nashville is where I belong.

I sit down and think of the journal in my purse and the words on the pages, Allison's words. Many times, I've felt like our lives shadowed one another, and I still want to believe that to be true. I want to believe that Tyler was her Brandon and she left Nashville with her true love. Tyler is many things, but he is no Brandon. And if Allie left Nashville, her cellphone did not. I shiver and hug myself.

CHAPTER THIRTY-FIVE

I finally get a moment to myself, so I shut my door and make a call I've been wanting to make. I dial Queen Compton. She answers on the first ring. "Allie, honey. Can I just say I adore your mother as much as I do you?"

She sounds stronger than I expect and this pleases me. "I'm not surprised," I say. "You're both fighters. Strong independent women."

"I hope you remember that lesson for the entirety of your life. I hear you're opening new doors for Riptide. I'm pleased."

This comment pleases *me*, but it also punches me in the gut. I mean, how do I leave Riptide when she has been so kind to me?

"Tell me about it."

We chat a bit about what I'm doing and she offers ideas. When we're about to hang up, she says, "My message to you: take control of your life."

I frown, remembering those words from a book, maybe? "Isn't that a quote from—I can't quite remember who, but it's a quote, I think?"

"It is," she confirms. "The great basketball player Charles Barkley. Everything smart doesn't have to come from a book. It usually comes from experience that we don't always have ourselves. We have but one life to live, and those around us have much to offer. I'm going to go lay down because apparently beating cancer's ass means sleeping way too much. I really hate being in bed."

"You'll be roaring through the halls of Riptide soon."

"Yes, I will. You'd be good to also remember those three words. Bye for now, Allie."

"Bye, Queen Compton."

She laughs. "Queen Compton?"

"Oops. Did I say that out loud?"

"Yes, you did, my dear."

"Well, now you know how I think of you. As the queen."

She laughs. "Bye, Allie." This time she disconnects.

"My message to you: take control of your life," I whisper.

In other words, I can allow myself to be boxed in or I can take control. I choose the latter. Instead of waiting for life to shape me, perhaps for the first time since I dared to move to New York City, I decide to take things into my own hands. I punch in Mark's number.

He answers on the first ring. "Ms. Wright. I do believe I've talked to you more since you moved to Nashville than I ever did when you were in New York."

"I know. That is true." I draw and breath and blurt out, "What if I want to stay here, work for Riptide, but not for Hawk?"

"You can contract scout for us. What else?"

"That's it? Yes?"

"Yes. That's one lesson my mother clearly hasn't taught you well. You get nothing you don't ask for. Consider this your job interview. You passed."

My eyes water a bit, and I don't know why. Joy, I think. "I might stay with Hawk. He's trying to get me to quit Riptide. And I promised you loyalty."

"And now you've given it. Loyalty is rewarded. Anything else?"

"Thank you. And that's all."

"Goodbye, Ms. Wright." He disconnects.

My lips slowly curve. The queen has spoken and for once, I think she's me.

CHAPTER THIRTY-SIX

I'm behind my desk at almost six o'clock when Dash calls. "How soon are you getting out of there, baby?"

"Quickly, I hope."

"What about the work-from-home situation we talked about?"

"I'm going to deal with it tomorrow. I've truly had way too much of the Hawk family today."

"The Hawk *family*?"

"Hawk Senior was in Tyler's office when I went to talk to him about the half-day thing and just in general wanted to tell him no to a lot of things."

"The word no when directed at Tyler sounds beautiful."

I laugh. "Beautiful?"

"It's pretty damn near."

I laugh again. "I'll leave in the next half hour. You want me to just come home or go to the bookstore?"

"I'll come to you."

"Sounds good."

"See you soon, cupcake."

"See you soon."

We disconnect and I smile over the "cupcake" endearment. If anyone told me I'd love being called cupcake before I met Dash, I'd have laughed. But it's our thing. It's reminiscent of how we met. And I love it. So much.

Eager to get out of here, I send Katie home, organize my desk, make some notes and damn it, the journal is sitting in my drawer. I just can't help myself. I open it to a random page.

Tonight, he seduced me. The funny thing is that yes, we had crazy, wild, intense sex—more on that later—but it was also romantic. He took me to dinner. We talked and talked. He opened up to me in a way he has never opened up. He told me how his father has controlled his life. He told me why he's so against marriage. His own parents don't exactly have a stellar relationship. His father controls him. His mother controls his father. He controls everything around him but his parents. I can't pretend to know what that's like, but what I care about is what it's like for him. And my doorbell just rang. More later...

I consider that passage and what it says about Tyler. I can definitely feel those words in the encounters I've had with both men. Interesting though that his mother left the company when she wants to control her husband. I flip to another random page further back, closer to that ominous final entry and my heart thunders in my chest at the first two words: *Dash Black.*

Dash Black.

I saw him today for the first time since THAT night. What can I say? Yes, he's hot. Yes, he's talented. Yes, he changed my life. But not in a good way.

He made secrets feel like they needed to stay secrets. He made being humans appear dangerous, not real. He hurt me and I haven't been in the same room as him for more than about a half-hour of my life. After THAT night, that miserable night, everything changed. I should probably write about it, but it's hard to even think about. Did Dash mean to hurt me? No. But I still can't forgive him. I just can't.

My hand is trembling because even though I'd know what night she's talking about even if Dash hadn't told me, I'd think there was more to it. And it's hard to hear Allison blame Dash for her split with Tyler. Tyler wasn't able to break up me and Dash. Neither of us let that happen. But Tyler let it happen with Allison.

"I see you're working late, Ms. Wright."

My gaze lifts to find Tyler standing in my doorway, one shoulder hitched on the frame. In that moment, I see what it was that Allison saw in Tyler. He's a beautiful man. His jaw strong, his face handsome, his body fit. His energy is all power and masculinity. And deep in his striking eyes, I can see what I didn't always see in Tyler. Dash described him as "fucked up." I'll just call him a tormented man. And I don't always like how that torment influences my life and career.

It's then that I realize the journal is open on my desk, in plain sight, and if anyone would know who it belongs to, it would be Tyler.

"You have something to say to me, Ms. Wright?"

The "Ms. Wright" is what triggers me. I shut the journal, stick it in my drawer and I don't just stand up. I walk around my desk and stand in front of him. "Allie," I snap. "My name is Allie. And since you have inserted yourself into my personal life, and I guess to some extent I have yours, we are borderline friends. Therefore, I will say this. You know what your problem is?"

He arches a brow. God, he reminds me of Mark at times. "Why do I know what you're about to tell me?" he asks dryly.

"You use things like 'Ms. Wright' to shut people out when they get too close to you. And don't tell me that's just business because we both know it runs deeper than that. For whatever reason, you don't trust people. Well, you can trust me, but you need to make sure I can trust you. While you try to protect yourself, you don't always protect those around you. You hurt them. Speaking of which, do something to make-up with Dash. And I'm not going to work for you, ever. If you want me to stay, I'll stay on as an employee of Riptide only. I hope you can live with that because I want to be here. And—that's all."

His lips twitch. "I do believe I didn't give you credit where credit is due, Allie. You can stay on at Riptide. Goodnight." He starts to back out of the office.

"Don't leave," I order.

He turns back to me, that eyebrow raised. "Yes, Allie?"

"She loved you, Tyler. *Really* loved you. If you love her—"

"I do," he shocks me by saying, his voice raw, gravelly. "But it's too late."

With that, he leaves, and there's no calling him back.

CHAPTER THIRTY-SEVEN

When I exit the building, Dash immediately pulls me into his arms, walks me out of the doorway, and kisses me until I'm too hot to feel the cold. "What was that for?" I ask when we come up for air. "You know people follow you with cameras?"

"I don't give two shits what people do. Just you. I missed you today."

My lips curve of their own compulsion. "You just saw me a couple hours ago."

"I know. It's kind of crazy. I never missed anyone in a couple hours before you, Allie."

"If you're trying to sweep me off my feet, Mr. Black, you had me at cupcake."

He laughs, low and sexy. "Is that right?"

"Yes," I say and just when I'm about to tell him all my news about my job, Mark, Tyler, and even Queen Compton, we hear, "What are you two doing?"

At the sound of Bella's voice, we break apart and she grins at us. "I do love you two love birds." She sighs. "One day maybe I'll meet someone as wonderful as Dash who is not my brother. For now, you two have to keep me company."

It's right then that cameras do indeed start flashing. Wonderful. Dash motions us to the door and in a crush of people we step inside, where Bella motions to a security guard. Dash calls for a car, and the three of us stand there, watching the building staff handle the problem.

Bella glances at me. "Wait until the next book, movie, or TV show."

LISA RENEE JONES

I eye Dash and he nods. "She's right. But it comes in waves. Today that article was the trigger."

Bella grins. "Because my brother is famous." She glances at me and moves seamlessly to another topic. "What do I bring for Thanksgiving?"

"Oh, please," I say. "Nothing. My mom goes way overboard with food."

"Well, what does she like? I'll bring a gift."

"Candles. She loves candles."

"Candles it is." She smiles.

A thought has me looking at Dash. "What if they got pictures of us kissing?"

"I'm sure they did. And why does it matter? The world knows we're together now, Allie."

"Woo," Bella says. "I hope Brandon sees and eats his little heart out."

Exactly where my head is at right now. Brandon is not a man to be goaded and take it well.

"Our car is here," Dash says, "and so is yours, Bella."

Bella waves to the guard and with his help and that of a police officer, we exit the building as a couple of reporters shout questions at Dash. Once we're in the car, which is not an Uber but a private hire, Dash says, "Home, Evans."

"You got it, Dash." The man eyes me over the seat. "Evening."

I greet him and sink into the leather seat. Dash tangles his fingers with mine and says, "He's handled, baby. I promise."

He reads me even better than I read one of his brilliant novels. I touch his cheek. "I hope so."

He kisses my hand. "He's handled," he repeats. His confidence is contagious, and I choose to believe him. Because I trust Dash. And because today is the day I choose to be happy.

CHAPTER THIRTY-EIGHT

Dash and I enter *our* apartment and he helps me with my coat and bag, shrugs out of his own coat, and then just that fast, I'm against the door and he's kissing me. God, how he's kissing me. Deep strokes of his tongue, the press of his hands on my body, the press of his hips to my hips, his erection against my belly.

"Did I mention how much I wanted to be inside you all afternoon?" he asks, his eyes heavy-lidded, his voice rough with desire. "Did I mention how much I *always* want to be inside you?"

"No, but feel free to show me," I say, and that's exactly what he does.

My shirt is off in a blink and so is his. Thick-roped muscle teases my hands. My bra is dragged down, his eyes ravishing my exposed breasts, my puckered nipples. He drags my skirt up my hips and in a rush of us both grabbing at his pants, they're down. We don't stop until we're both naked, until my leg is at his hip and he's pressing inside me, thick, hard, and oh so good. I'm panting when he cups my face and says, "He's never going to hurt you again."

"I'm not worried about me. I'm worried about you."

"Good. You're mine now."

I smile and say, "Yes. Yes, I am."

I'd tell him he's mine, too, but he's kissing me again, cupping my backside and driving into me, him at my front, the door at my back. Our breathing fills the room. His hair wraps my fingers. Sensations rock my body.

Dash shifts and turns me, walking toward the couch, where he sits down and then I'm on top of him. I'm straddling him, my hands catching on his shoulders, fingers flexing. Our eyes lock, and he says, "God, woman why do you always make me feel like I've been waiting for this all my life?" He cups my head and drags my mouth closer. "I'm yours too, Allie. You know that, right?"

There are times when I think Dash will never be all mine, and another woman isn't the problem. His self-hate is, but right now is not one of those moments. There is a pull between us, magnetic, intense, and I whisper, "Yes," overwhelmed with all the crazy sensations this man makes me feel.

I press my lips to his and he moans, a low, rough masculine sound, his tongue a sultry slide against my tongue, and then we are swaying, moving together, loving and fucking, and all over each other. A rush of movement. Then slow. Fast. Repeat. Our lips part, our breaths mingling, before we erupt into wildness again. And I don't want this to end. I don't want it to end. Ever. I don't want anything but him and us, and yes, forever with Dash. But even if we are forever, this cannot be. Passion roars between us and the fierceness of our need for each other and ultimate satisfaction can only be tamed so long. Dash drags me down and thrusts hard. My body spasms around him. I tumble into one of the most intense, body-quaking orgasms of my life.

I bury my face in his shoulder. He wraps his arm around my waist, thrusting again, a low, rough, aroused sound sliding from his lips as he quakes beneath me.

Clinging to him, I'm panting and he's panting as we collapse into each other, our bodies intimately close. As time comes back to me, my mind begins to replay all that happened today and I want him to know everything, and I want him to know now. "I went to see Tyler," I say, and when I would push back to look at him, he has already reacted.

"Do not say that man's name while I'm inside you, Allie." He rolls me to my back, reaches to the end table, and hands me a tissue.

"Dash."

"I'm serious, Allie. Bad fucking timing. Take it," he says of the tissue.

He's angry and I feel horrible. He's right. I just really blew a special moment I was trying to make more special, but he's being ultra-sensitive about Tyler as well. I quickly grab the tissue, and stuff it between my legs the best I can. He's already moving off of me, sitting up and I sit up, too, but I take it one step further. I slide off the couch to my knees in front of him. "Sorry. That was the wrong thing to start with. I was going to say—well, let me backtrack completely. Today I realized that you never asked me to leave New York or my job for you. You were willing to go there for me. I'm leaving because it's what I want. I'm not going to ask you to leave Nashville for me, even part of the time."

"I would do anything for you, Allie. You know that."

Relief washes over me at that remark that says he's mad, but still present. "Yes," I say. "I do know. And that you would means the world to me. So back to what I was trying to tell you and did so badly. Tyler said I need to be in or out, with my job and you. That wasn't bad advice. He was right about that, Dash, but you know my response. I said to him, I'm all in *with Dash*. I'm all in and I want you to know that. Home is with you."

He softens his shoulders, his expression, his voice, but I hold up a hand. "Listen, please. I called Mark today. He offered to let me stay on as a contract scout. I told Tyler he either lets me work for Riptide or I won't work for Hawk Legal anymore at all. He agreed to let me stay on as a member of Riptide. I'm not sure after today how much working at home I can do for this tightly scheduled auction, but after this auction, things change. I'm going to try and make that be a remote job, working from home or with you wherever we need to travel, if you want me to travel with you," I add quickly.

Dash lifts me back onto his lap, straddling me, his hand pressed between my shoulder blades. "I always want you with me, but are you sure this is what you want?"

"Very, very sure. I'm sorry I said Tyler's name. I was just excited to tell you everything and for once he said something that felt right."

"I overreacted. I'm sorry for that and I'm sorry for a lot of things, baby. Everything in New York. That night here. Hell yes, travel with me. *Stay* with me."

"That means the good, bad, and ugly, Dash."

"I know that, baby. I'm all in, just like you, but I don't promise you I won't want to fight. I just promise you, this time, I'll choose you."

And for the first time, I believe I've seen enough for him to let me see the worst. When the time is right, and there will be a right time, we'll ride out the storm together.

CHAPTER THIRTY-NINE

The next day I meet Millie Roberts from the charity for coffee at her office to discuss the guestlist for the auction, invitations, and much more. It's near noon when I arrive at the office and as William Shakespeare said, "*Better three hours too soon than a minute too late.*" I feel late today, anxious to get things moving.

"Oh my God, Allie," is how Katie greets me, and does so looking adorable in a polka-dotted blouse and a flared skirt. "The donations keep coming in but we don't have time to validate them."

"November fifteenth is the cutoff date for this year," I say, finally sitting down behind my desk for the first time today, "and even that's pushing it," I add. "Let them know that I'll now be handling year-round auctions for the charity or otherwise. I can personally call everyone who needs one-on-one attention, but try and get me as many details as you can on what they're looking to auction."

"Wait," Katie says, her eyes lighting up. "You're staying? Tell me you're staying here with us?"

"I am staying," I confirm, "but I'll be back on the Riptide payroll as of January one, working here with Hawk Legal and their clients." *I hope that's how this works*, I think silently, but decide I'll figure it out later. Someone will pay me. I'm really not worried about that particular point.

"So, you're basically working for Riptide *and* Hawk. My God, talk about a dream job." She does this little bow thing over and over and backs out of the office with a grin, as she adds. "Queen Allie."

No, I think. I am not the queen. That title is taken and well deserved. But this *is* a dream job and I made it happen. I'm proud of myself. And on that note, being a protégée to said queen has worked up an appetite. I'm starving—quite literally my stomach is growling. Having already warned Dash I have to stay in today for lunch, I scoop up some work and head to the cafeteria. It's a good half hour later when I'm at a table, scarfing my food, and pecking away at my keyboard when someone sits down in front of me. I blink with the realization that it's Benjamin.

"Hello, Allison," he says.

As with yesterday, his suit is expensive, and his eyes are a bit too probing. The crinkles by his eyes and the gray in his dark hair I'd been too busy guarding the journal last time to notice tell me he's mid-forties not mid-thirties. Not that the gray doesn't suit him. Men always get away with that older, distinguished, worldly look, while women just get out the hair dye. Or we don't know we're gray because we already had out the hair dye and we'd prefer it that way.

"Allie," I say. "Call me Allie."

"I've asked my secretary, Jessica, to get in touch with you this afternoon and offer her aid. I'm going to be traveling soon while she is not."

"That's really not necessary."

"And yet, it is," he says. "I must admit I'm intrigued by the auction. This is not something we've done for our clients in the past. Last year was an informal event and we certainly didn't have Riptide involved. On that note, I'll also admit I'd like to be a part of what I believe to be a leg up for Hawk Legal. This is a service no one else is offering their clients. That we're partnering with Riptide means it's not likely to be duplicated."

"You know about Riptide," I comment.

"I've been asking questions since meeting you, Allie. I won't get that wrong again. No more Allison. You might look like her, but you most definitely are not her."

My brows furrow. "What does that mean?"

"Well, for one thing, she's gone, and I understand you'll be staying."

"Most people are surprised she's gone."

"I'm not," he says. "Not at all." His cellphone rings and he pulls back his jacket, snagging his phone from an inner pocket. After a glance at the caller ID, he says, "Gotta take this. It's a studio exec." He winks and gives me a two-finger wave, and then he's on his feet, answering his call, and walking away.

I watch him leave and wonder why he isn't surprised that Allison is gone when everyone else seems to be. Well, except Tyler, who was sleeping with her. I grab my phone and text Dash: *Any word from Neil? Especially on Benjamin? I just had a weird encounter with him.*

Dash calls me. I answer and he says, "Do you know how much I don't want you in that place right now?"

"I wouldn't know you if it weren't for this place."

"But you do now. What happened?"

I replay the conversation. He's silent a moment and then says, "I haven't heard from Neil, but I left him a message this morning."

"What do you think?"

"I don't like any of it, Allie."

"We're doing good things to help people, Dash—you and me and the charity."

"I'll happily donate whatever you think the auction will make to get you out of this."

"Up to five hundred thousand."

"Okay. I'll write the damn check."

I sometimes forget how rich Dash is because he doesn't flaunt his money. "It's only a month, Dash. After that, I can work from home, at least most of the time. And hopefully, Neil will find Allison." I glance up to find Katie walking toward me. "Katie is looking panicked. I need to go."

"Be careful, baby."

"I will. I promise."

We say a quick goodbye, and disconnect just as Katie sits down in front of me and starts rambling about a difficult client who's a country singer. "I'll call him. I'll handle it."

"You're so comfortable with these high-profile people. I guess because you're seeing Dash Black, right?"

Obviously, that's a topic she really wanted to bring up. "I live with Dash, Katie."

Her eyes go wide. "You live with him?"

"Yes. I do. It's new, but pretty wonderful."

"Oh my God." She holds her heart. "You're like Cinderella."

I laugh. "No. I'm not. And believe me, just because someone is famous does not make them Prince Charming. My father is someone famous and he's definitely not."

"Who is he?"

"Enough about me for one day," I say, shifting topics. "What do you know about Benjamin?"

"Not much. He's nice enough, I guess. Some of the agents are not, but he's nice to the staff. Why?"

"He's going to have his secretary offer to help us. Do we want her help?"

"I don't know her, but usually if someone is a bitch that gets around. I think we can use the help. Are you okay with that?"

"Maybe. Let me think about what we could give away safely. What was his involvement with Allison?"

"I didn't know they had any. Why do you ask that?"

"He said he wasn't surprised she was gone, but I didn't get more out of him."

She frowns. "What did he know that the rest of us didn't?"

Exactly, I think. Exactly.

LISA RENEE JONES

CHAPTER FORTY

Dash wakes the next morning inspired by the storyline of Ghost in an underground fight club, apparently *really* inspired, because he brushes his teeth, kisses me, and then goes hunting for his MacBook. I head to the bathroom, shower, and dress in a belted navy-blue dress. I've already finished getting ready for the day and there is no sign of Dash. A little concerned something is going on, I grab my things and head toward the living room to find him sitting at the kitchen island, pounding away on his keyboard. Of course, he's still in his pajama bottoms and a snug white T-shirt stretched across his impressive chest, but it doesn't make him look hot. He makes *it* look hot.

I sit down beside him and sip from his cup. "You really are inspired," I comment.

"That's how it happens for me. In waves. Therefore, me and the coffee pot are cozying up right here at this counter today," he says, but his mind, at least for the moment, is no longer on his work.

He reaches for my mug, his eyes meeting mine as he presses his mouth to the exact spot I've just sipped, the intimacy of us sharing that coffee doing funny things to my belly. We live together now, I know, but all these little things that become "us" things are new to me. Yes, I was engaged to Brandon, but there was nothing remotely familiar about that and this.

"Morning. baby," he murmurs, as if to say, this is a breather, a moment for us.

"Good morning, Dash," I say, smiling. "I can't wait to read the book."

"Soon," he promises. "Very soon."

LISA RENEE JONES

"Since you're inspired to finish up, should I bring you lunch?"

He sets the cup down and rotates to face me, mischief lighting his eyes, a one-day sexy stubble shadowing his jaw. "Will you have time to be naked?"

I laugh. "No, and neither will you. You're inspired and should stay that way. I'll send lunch."

"Probably a good idea, though I like the part where you're my lunch much better."

I smile and kiss his cheek. "I'll tell Bella not to bug you today."

"Now that is a good idea, if I ever heard one," he agrees. "If she asks me my word count one more time, I'm going to stop taking her calls."

I laugh and leave the house feeling happier than I remember ever feeling and why wouldn't I be? Watching Dash work is a bit like watching the wonder of a rainbow streaking the blue sky with colors. Everything about his process, from his facial expressions while he types, the intensity of his keystrokes, to the gallons of coffee he drinks, intrigues me. He hasn't asked me to read his work again and I have a feeling that's a good sign. This book is going to be brilliant. He needs no validation.

Once I'm in the elevator I text Bella: *Dash is still in his pajamas writing. If he can stay in his zone maybe you'll get that book early.*

In other words, she answers, *don't call him and tell him that one of the studios wants to come here to meet him.*

Not if you want the book early, I reply.

Okay, so you tell him. It's Nick Snyder. He wants to come next Tuesday, she replies.

I'll tell him, I promise.

The elevator dings and I slide my phone into my bag before exiting and cutting right to the lobby. That's

186

where a short woman in a fitted cream-colored dress that I'm quite certain is Chanel, turns to greet me. "You must be Allie," she says. "I'm Jessica, Benjamin's assistant. He's officially out of town for a couple of weeks. I'm at your service."

Jessica is short, full-figured, and has waves of blonde curly hair with freckled cheeks that she pairs with impeccable style. She's also friendly enough and I don't feel I can really turn down help right now. Not when it appears to be more than talk.

I chat with her a bit and we head to my office.

Much later, she and I are sitting together at a table in the cafeteria, sipping coffee and going over the auction details, I use the time to do a little digging. "I can't believe Benjamin could spare you."

"He's actually a really generous person. He's arrogant and a bit of a show-off, but absolutely a good guy."

"Your help is appreciated. Allison leaving so abruptly took everyone off guard and left me chasing a fast deadline. Well, except Benjamin. He told me it didn't surprise him."

"Really? What did he say?"

"Just that. He wasn't surprised. He didn't elaborate. Maybe they had a personal relationship."

"I doubt it. He's into blondes. And I usually know the flavor of the day. He does run through the women. I've found him to simply have a good read on people. Obviously, he believes you're going to be staying around because I'm here, helping you. He didn't have me help Allison."

"Yes, well, she had a bit more time than me to plan this."

Her brows knit. "It *is* curious that she left. She had a lot of buzz in the firm like she was climbing the ladder."

She snorts. "She probably left for a man, right? It's always a man." Katie chooses then to join us and the conversation is over, at least, on the topic of Allison.

CHAPTER FORTY-ONE

I order food for Dash for lunch, but I don't call him for fear of breaking his concentration. I'm stuffing a salad in my face when he instead calls me. "Neil is meeting with Tyler today, right now actually," he informs me. "Tyler is giving him the security footage from the house you and Allison stayed in."

"That's good news, right?"

"It's something to work with," he says, "though Tyler told him he's been through it all, even the footage for the office."

"So not much help," I comment, feeling a bit defeated when it comes to the hunt for Allison. "What about Benjamin? Was he personally involved with Allison?"

"Outside of them sharing a few calls and text messages, still nothing significant."

"He sent his assistant to help as promised. She sings his praises and says that if Benjamin knew what others did not about Allison, then he's just a perceptive guy. I don't buy it. To me, if he knew more about her than anyone else, then the communication, no matter how minor it might have seemed, might be significant, right?"

"Neil looked at the dates of the communications and they occurred weeks before she seems to have disappeared."

"Oh. Well, that doesn't seem to be leading where I was thinking it might. So now what?"

"Let Neil keep digging, baby, but this isn't always a fast process. And Benjamin wasn't the only person who knew Allison wasn't going to stay at Hawk Legal. Tyler knew."

"Right," I say, but I resist going down that rabbit hole. "Is Benjamin close to Tyler? Could he have known something about Allison through Tyler?"

"No."

When we hang up, I repeat two words in my mind: *Tyler knew.*

My gut twists in a tight knot.

***

That night I work late, stuck on the phone with more than one of the Hawk clients donating to the auction. When I finally leave, it's at Dash's prodding. He calls and I answer to hear, "I'm coming to get you and I'm not taking no for an answer."

My lips curve and I say, "Well, if you're not taking no for an answer—"

"Good. I'm already walking in that direction."

"I'll meet you in the lobby."

We disconnect and I load my bag, slide it on my shoulder, and I'm ready to leave. Exiting my office, I walk through the dark hallways and hit the button for the elevator. It's a bit spooky and I'm more than a little relieved to have the doors open fairly instantly. I step inside the empty car and it hangs, kind of like the ones in horror movies, when the girl is trying to escape the monster, but slowly begins to close.

It's almost there when a male hand catches one side and it jerks back open.

I hold my breath, my heart racing as Tyler appears in the opening.

I'm both relieved and on edge.

He joins me, punching the lobby button I've already pushed, for good measure. We turn to face each other and tension pulses between us. I flash back to the night I ended up in a car with his father, and I decide that while, yes, this is awkward, it's different. Tyler is someone I know. His father is someone I don't know.

"You think something happened to her," he says, his voice tight as a whip.

Obviously, his communication with Neil brought us to this conversation. "I told you I was worried. I asked you to worry with me."

"What if she just doesn't want to be found? She hates me. I told you that."

"Aren't you giving yourself too much credit, Tyler? I have her journal and while, yes, she loved you, *loves* you," I amend, "she was, *is,* a strong independent woman. Maybe she just had enough of not being enough for you."

His expression tightens. "That was her journal on your desk. You have her journal."

It's not a question, but I answer anyway. "Yes. I have it."

"And?"

"She got involved with someone after you. She thought it was a mistake. She feared it was a problem. And the entries end abruptly. Do you know who it was?"

"Brad Waters. She was involved with him."

"Let's hope it's not him because he's looking for her, too. You know that. He came here to find her. Who else could it have been?"

"I have no idea," he says tightly, "but it seems clear to me that if I don't know where she is and he doesn't know where she is, she chose to leave."

"Why do you keep going back to that?" I demand, starting to get angry with him. "Why can't you worry about her with me? *Why* can't you see another possibility other than her leaving so that you can help us find her?"

"*Ms. Wright,*" he snaps.

"Allie."

"You're asking me to consider the idea that something happened to her, that she's no longer on this earth. In other words, I drove her in the wrong direction, I let her go, I pushed her to what became her *fucking* demise. And so, you have your answer. *That's* why I'm not willing to consider anything but she left because she wanted to leave. Do you understand me?"

At this point, he's close, really close and I don't even know when the door opened, but it's open.

"Allie," Dash says softly, apparently having witnessed at least part of this from outside the car.

Tyler grits his teeth and turns, his eyes meeting Dash's for an intense moment before he exits the car, cutting left toward the garage elevators. I exit and step in front of Dash, his hands sliding to my waist, warm and protective, which feels really nice right about now.

"What was that?" he asks.

"He's afraid Allison is gone, Dash. Really gone."

A chill races down my spine and back up again because I am, too.

CHAPTER FORTY-TWO

On the Tuesday of the next week, I work late, while Dash has drinks with a group of studio execs intent on winning his TV show rights. It's really looking as if by Thanksgiving, which is fast approaching, Dash should have a home for his TV show. I'm actually eager to get home to be there when he returns to hear all the news. Bella plans to come over for the same reason.

I'm just thinking about packing up, when to my shock, Jack—Hawk Senior—appears in my doorway. "Oh good, I caught you. I have some people I want you to meet. Meet me on the rooftop in fifteen, will you?" He doesn't wait for an answer.

Nerves assail me. What the heck is this? I text Bella: *Jack just told me to meet him on the rooftop. There are people he wants me to meet.*

I know he had a couple of record producers in today, she replies. *Maybe he's involving them in the auction.*

Maybe. I don't know. It's a little unexpected. I'll meet you at the house. Just let yourself in.

I always do, she jokes, because yes, she does. She caught me in my bra and panties this past weekend when she showed up at the apartment unexpectedly.

Nervous about the unknown portion of this meeting, I fix my face and then head upstairs. As soon as I enter the rooftop room, I find a group of men at a table, the Nashville city lights twinkling through the nearby windows. Oh yes, this will be a brilliant place for the auction. I make a mental note to hire a photographer. How have I not handled that part of the party? And can I even get one this late?

Jack must spot me because he stands and motions me to the table. Before long, I'm sitting with a group of five men, all players in the music industry, talking about the auction. Thank you, Queen Compton, for preparing me for this with the hundreds of similar presentations she entrusted me with. When I've finished my pitch, I've received a twenty-thousand-dollar donation for the charity, and hold the cards of two men with pricey items they'd like to run through Riptide. I'm elated. Mark will be elated as well, but act as if he is not. That's Mark. It's kind of Tyler as well.

It's not, however, Jack. When the men leave, he raves. "You were brilliant. You got one of the stingiest guys in the business to write a check. You should be an agent."

"I've dealt with enough agents to know I don't want to be an agent. And you do know I'm going to stay on with Riptide, right?"

"But work here," he supplies, his intelligent eyes calculating in a way I can't quite size up. "I believe having Riptide on-site drives up our stock. They all knew you were a Riptide representative. You just helped me get the word out about our new partnership. How about I buy you a drink to celebrate?"

I'm sure this is just how Jack operates, but I have a funny feeling in my belly, and not funny in a good way.

"I actually have to be somewhere tonight." I glance at my watch and find it's almost eight. "I really need to head home. Thank you for the opportunity, Jack."

"My absolute pleasure, Allie." His cellphone rings and he snags it from his pocket, glances at the number, and then at me. "I'll stay up here and take this. Be careful going home."

"Thank you again." I hurry out of the room and to the elevators and I don't know why, but I feel uncomfortable when there is not one single reason I can find to feel anything but happy.

***

I arrive home to find Bella drinking wine and watching her father's race on the television. She has a glass waiting on me and fills it. It's not long until Dash is home and joining us. "They want Ryan Gosling to play Ghost," he says. "This isn't *The* fucking *Notebook*."

Bella and I laugh, and then I ask, "Who do you want to play Ghost?"

"An unknown," he says. "People need that person to be Ghost, not Ryan-fucking-Gosling. They need to be surprised by how much they love the guy." He leans in and whispers, "Like me with you." He kisses my neck.

Bella starts screaming as her dad crosses the finish line and I hop up to shout with her. Dash is laughing as she and I hug. Happy is the word of the night. I'm happy. I have no idea why I was feeling weird earlier, but it's most certainly past now.

After the race has ended, Bella, Dash, and I debate Dash's Hollywood options and Bella writes down points of negotiation. It's then that Dash receives a call, listens, and says little, as whoever it is talks to him. When he disconnects, Dash says, "Brandon just got on a plane. He's leaving. It's done." His hand is on my leg and he squeezes gently.

Bella beats me to the punch and asks what I would. "Are you sure?"

"One hundred percent sure," Dash confirms. "He was pushed out of the country and I promise you, he will not risk coming back."

"What did he do, Dash?" I press yet again when he's previously denied me that information. "I really need to know. Protecting me is great, the less I know, the less to incriminate myself—I get that. But I also need closure."

"Aside from stealing from his employer? Insider trading and not in a little way."

I don't ask more. On some level, I guess I knew he was a bad person and bad people do bad things.

Not long after that, Bella heads home and instead of Dash and I talking about Brandon, we talk through a bit of a plot issue he wrote himself into today. We got to bed in each other's arms, and in the middle of the darkness, he says. "I've never had anyone I'd plot with, Allie. No one."

But he does with me.

"I like it," he adds.

"I like it, too," I murmur, and I slowly slide into sleep, feeling safe—and yes, *happy*—in his arms.

CHAPTER FORTY-THREE

For the next two days, Dash is holed up at home working, still crunching the backend of his book. His goal is to be nearly done with the book by Thanksgiving and it appears he might just do it.

For me, those same next few days have me arriving to work feeling festive and excited. The auction is coming together. My life has come together. And my mother is so excited about seeing Keith Urban that it's fun just thinking about us all going together. For the most part, Tyler and I avoid each other, but with plans to leave early Friday for the concert, I decide I need to let him know.

With a peace offering, a vanilla cupcake in hand, I luck out to find his secretary gone to lunch—not that I planned it that way or anything like that. Trying to be respectful, I peek my head in and suck in a breath to find him and his father at his window again. *Damn it, no.* I try to back away and escape but I hear Tyler say, "Ms. Wright. Why are you scurrying about like a mouse?"

How did he know I was here?

He turns and so does his father, the two powerful, well-dressed, good-looking men filling the room up with enough testosterone to suffocate a poor little ol' girl like me. "I didn't mean to interrupt."

"I was just telling my son what a good eye he has for talent," Jack interjects. "Anyone who can get a tightwad to write a twenty-thousand-dollar check is a keeper. You're making him look good."

"What is it there you brought me?" Tyler queries, eyeing the small box in my hand.

"A cupcake."

His eyes dance with amusement. "You brought me a cupcake?"

"Yes. I heard assholes like cupcakes." It's out before I can stop it.

His father roars with laughter. Tyler surprises me and closes the small space between me and him, accepting the box. He glances at the cupcake and then me. "I've always enjoyed vanilla."

Somehow, I don't think he's talking about the cupcake, but I just called him an asshole in front of his father. I can't really say I don't deserve whatever he dishes out.

"Call me when you're done here, please?"

"Yes, Ms. Wright. I will absolutely call you."

With that, I back out of the room and hurry down the hallway, mentally face-palming.

***

It's about an hour later, as I stuff a bite of egg salad sandwich in my mouth, that Tyler appears in my doorway. Once again, I almost choke, and he watches in amusement. While I down water, trying to seem as if I look anything but silly, he steps inside the office and shuts the door.

"Why did I get a cupcake and an insult today, Ms. Wright?"

He's big and intimidating in my office with that door shut and I stand up, trying to even the playing field. "That was a sample of the cupcakes I'm about to invoice you to purchase for the event."

"You don't need my approval for cupcakes," he says.

"It's a lot of cupcakes. We have hundreds of people attending. Did you like it?"

"Yes. Vanilla is my favorite."

"Stop with the vanilla thing, Tyler. We both know your mind is in the gutter."

"Never, Ms. Wright. You're a taken woman and I am nothing if not honorable, contrary to anything Dash might have told you."

I ignore his comments. "I'm leaving a little early today."

"You don't need my permission for that, either. You work for Riptide."

"Not until January first," I say, referencing the memo I'd gotten from HR this morning. "Your HR person told me so by email today. My official employment with Hawk legal ends December thirty-first."

"Well then, I guess I still have a chance to keep you for myself."

"Tyler—"

"I'd still prefer you work for Hawk Legal, Allie."

"Why does it matter?"

"Because as long as you have one foot out the door, I'll always believe you're temporary. And maybe some part of you wants an exit."

I round the desk and just like I did once before, I stand in front of him. "Just because you're not completely in control doesn't mean this isn't good or right. I'm here. I'm not going anywhere. Not unless you push me out the door." I'm thinking about Allison and how he pushed her out the door.

And he knows. I see it in his eyes. He says, "And are you in control?" he challenges.

"I—I am."

"And Dash is what?"

"In control of himself."

"Exactly. I'm not under the illusion control cannot be shared. Are you?"

"No."

"Then perhaps control is not the problem here."
"Then what is?"
"The illusion of having what you do not."
And with that, he turns and leaves.

CHAPTER FORTY-FOUR

The illusion of having what you do not.
While I can see how they feel real to Tyler—he lost Allison—I am at a different place in life. I lived an illusion in New York. Brandon was an illusion, happiness was an illusion, but that's not the here and now, that is not the me of the present. For that reason, I set aside that encounter with Tyler and focus on a fun night with the man I love and my parents.

The concert arrives and it's a blast to attend. I don't remember the last time I saw my mother so happy. She sings along with Keith Urban, hugs my stepfather and me, and afterward, we finish the night at mine and Dash's apartment, where my mother raves about how beautiful it is. With Christmas music playing in the background, and coffees in hand, my mother and I sit by the fireplace and window, talking, as Dash and my stepfather do the same in the kitchen. Meanwhile, my father hasn't even bothered to return my calls and I don't know why I care. This is my family.

"You two are so cute together."

"I could say the same of you two," I tease her.

"There is something to be said for finding your soul mate, don't you think?"

I glance in Dash's direction and he just happens to be doing the same of me. He winks and my belly flutters.

"Oh my," my mother says. "The way he looks at you, honey. And the way you look at him."

I know the topic of marriage is about to come up and thankfully, I'm saved when my cellphone rings on the coffee table and Bella's number appears on the screen. I set my cup down and answer with a smile. "Hey. How was the race?"

"I need you to go to the bathroom and call me back and do not tell Dash it's me. Just pretend I'm a wrong number. Don't ask questions." She hangs up.

Unease rattles through me. "I need to go to the bathroom. Be right back."

My mom catches my arm. "What's wrong?"

"I don't know. Dash's sister wants me to go to the bathroom and call her and not let Dash know. She sounds shaken."

"Oh dear. Okay."

"If I come back and lift a finger, I need you to leave. Okay?"

"Yes. Of course. We'll go now."

"No. If I don't stay to say goodbye, Dash will feel something is off. I'll be right back."

She nods and I stand, avoiding Dash's gaze as I walk around the couches and hurry toward the bedroom. I step into the bathroom and into the toilet area and shut the door. I dial Bella. "I'm alone," I say, the minute she answers. "What is going on?"

"Dash's stepmom called me. It's really ridiculous she won't even call him, but in this case, I think it's for the best. His dad had a massive heart attack, Allie. He died."

My hand goes to my neck. "Died?"

"Yes. He's gone. And I'm not going to be able to get there until tomorrow. I can call and tell him or you can tell him. What do you want to do?"

Turn back time and make this go away, I think. "I'll tell him."

"His father's will says he doesn't want Dash at his funeral. The bastard had to hurt him one last time. He's going to want to fight, Allie."

"I know. I won't let him."

"I'm not sure you'll be able to stop him. I'm going to call Tyler. If he fights, Tyler can try to help shut it down."

"Do not let Tyler call or come over here."

"I won't. He's smarter than that."

She keeps talking, but I barely hear what she says. The storm is here and it's a big one.

CHAPTER FORTY-FIVE

Tears burn my eyes, knowing how much this is going to torment Dash, but I wipe them away.

He needs me to be strong.

I text my mother and tell her what's going on. She returns a message: *Oh my God. This is horrible. I'm going to go encourage your stepdad toward the door. Let me know how I can help when you have time to process everything.*

Drawing a deep breath, I walk back into the living room to find my mother and stepfather gathering their coats. I hurry forward and give my mother a hug. She whispers in my ear, "Just hold him really hard, honey."

I nod and as she steps away from me, Dash slides his arm around my shoulders. My mother and stepfather depart and Dash locks up. My stomach is in knots, literally twisting and turning, and I'm so nervous my chest hurts. Dash turns to face me and the minute he looks at me, he says, "What's wrong?"

"I have some bad news. I don't know how to tell you this. I don't *want* to tell you this."

He pales. "Bella—"

"She's fine," I say quickly. "She's trying to get on an earlier flight to get here."

"Allie, what's going on?" I close the space between us and when I would hug him, he catches my shoulders. "What's going on?"

"Your father—"

"What did he do now?"

"Died, Dash. He died." The words quake from my mouth. "He had a massive heart attack and he's—*gone.*"

His expression hardens, but his jaw and his hands tremble. "He's dead," he repeats.

"And because I think you need to hear all the bad at once, and I hope I'm right about that—"

"You are. Say it."

"He doesn't want you at the funeral. It's in his will."

He flinches. "How did you find this out?"

"Your stepmom called Bella."

"Of course she did. She can't even talk to me." He releases me and runs a rough hand over his jawline. "I need out of here." He turns toward the door.

I'm between it and him in a blink. "No." My hands plant on his chest. "We both know what happens when you go out that door, Dash. Stay with me."

"I need air, Allie. Walk with me."

The illusion of having what you do not.

I'm about to find out if those words apply to me and Dash. "If you go out the door, even with me by your side, I won't be able to control what comes next. I'm begging you to hold onto me the way I want to hold onto you right now. Use me however you want. Use me, Dash."

His jaw is set hard, his eyes half-veiled, seconds ticking by before he takes a wide step backward. "Undress, Allie."

The command is unexpected and I can't help but feel a bit vulnerable myself right now. "While you're still dressed?"

"Yes."

"Are you going to leave?"

He's back in front of me, hands on my arms, dragging me to him. "Do you think I'd do that to you, Allie? Tell me you don't."

"No," I say, "but you're grieving Dash. You both loved and hated him and that's about as confusing and brutal as it gets. No one is the same in those circumstances."

"I'm still me," he says. "The same me that fucked up with you in the past, but I promised you it wouldn't happen again. I'm damn sure not losing you over him."

My heart swells with his emotionally packed vow. "You aren't losing me."

He strokes my hair. "Then undress, Allie."

I nod and he releases my arms. I lean against the door and pull off the combat-style boots I'd changed into before the concert. Next, come my jeans and socks. Then my T-shirt and bra and underwear. When I'm naked, my eyes meet his and what I find is turbulence, pain, and anger, but there is also this unexpected wave of tenderness that is somehow just as intense as all those other emotions.

Dash moves then, scooping me up and carrying me toward the living room. I cling to him, not sure what to expect right now. He sets me on my feet in front of the couch and he sits. His hands are on my hips when he leans forward and kisses my belly. I expected a wild, dominant side of Dash, especially after he had me undress. My fingers slide into his hair and he looks up at me, pure torment in his eyes. For reasons I can't explain, I know that this isn't about wild, intense fucking. Dash feels naked, more naked than simply taking off his clothes would make him.

"He hated me because I was at the same party as my brother and I didn't stop my brother from getting in the car."

"He was an adult, Dash. Surely your father knew that."

"My brother did this all the time. He got drunk. He forced me to babysit him. I'd tried to get him in rehab. Hell, Bella tried, too, and Alex wasn't even her brother. We both told my father and my stubborn ass stepmother that he needed rehab. No one listened. That night I'd had enough. I was a college kid, Allie. There was this hot chick I wanted to bang and she was with me. I told Alex just to go ahead and get in the fucking car and drive. I was in an upstairs frat house bedroom fucking that chick whose name I can't even remember when my brother hit that tree." He drags me onto his lap, my legs straddling his hips, and his head buried against my neck, arms around my waist.

He holds me, his body quaking, my hand on the back of his head. "It wasn't your responsibility to save him, Dash."

He pulls back and looks at me, his eyes bloodshot. "Then who else was going to save him?" His voice rasps with emotion.

"Him," I say. "He had to make the decision to get help. Just like you need to choose something other than fighting."

"I did choose," he says softly, roughly. "I chose you."

"And I chose you. None of this even comes close to changing that."

He pulls my mouth to his and then we're kissing, a kiss that is passion, pain, and tenderness, and yet, it's wild and full of demand. I tug his shirt over his head and he tosses it away, standing with me to undress. And when we come back together, me on top, the thick ridge of his erection pressed inside me, there is vulnerability between us. We are exposed in every way together, and it's the most beautiful, wildly passionate experience of my life. Dash's hands and mouth are all over my body and mine are all over his.

Much later when we lay on the couch, our naked bodies entwined, Dash does what he has never done. He tells me stories about his brother—happy, funny stories—but there are none of his father, which hurts my heart. At some point, we fall asleep and I wake to Dash inside me again, making love to me. Afterward, he carries me to the bed, and I'm relieved when he falls asleep next to me, his breathing steady.

The storm has withdrawn, at least for tonight, but tomorrow is a new day.

We wake the next morning to Bella knocking on the door. The minute Dash sees her, he hugs her and she hugs him. Her eyes meet mine in the midst of his embrace, and she must sense that he's okay, because she whispers, "Thank you."

We head to the kitchen, where Bella promises us a feast. It's about that time that Tyler sends me a text: *How is he?*

I reply with: *Sorrowful and hopeful, but he's okay. We are getting through it.*

We exchange a few more messages and I put my phone away, joining Dash and Bella at the kitchen island.

Waffles and coffee follow and as Dash tells Bella a few of the stories he told me, I realize that in some ways he never grieved for his brother. Somehow losing his father has brought forth a need to grieve both men. And with that genuine grief, he's healing.

But Tyler was also right. The illusion of having what you do not is real.

In Dash's case, that was responsibility for his brother's death. Inexplicably, somehow, it's his father who both created that illusion and now has torn it away. How? I do not know, but he was Dash's father, and no matter what, losing him is painful. Perhaps surviving that means Dash must forgive himself for what his father could not.

LISA RENEE JONES

CHAPTER FORTY-SIX

A private memorial service, rather than a funeral, will be held for Dash's father after the New Year. Dash is still not invited. I suspect this was a decision his stepmother made to avoid the bad press over Dash not being present. The delay allows the "story" in the press to fade and become less interesting. I think it helps soften Dash's discomfort over not attending as well, which is a blessing. He's struggled with his father's death, but seems fairly okay right now, but then, Dash *always* seems fairly okay, even when he's not. For that reason, I spend most of the next week at home with Dash and do so with Tyler's vote of approval.

The film people give him a breather that he needs as well, and Dash dives into his book, determined to make that finish line goal of Thanksgiving. I decide it's the escape from the real world he needs. But he also jogs a lot, which means so do I. I figure it's a great way to get ready for our Thanksgiving feast, which will be worth every mile needed to pay for it. My mom's a nurse, Ms. Watch Your Cholesterol herself, but when it comes to the holidays, healthy isn't even in the vocabulary.

It's Thanksgiving eve when Bella stops with a bottle of wine with an offer from the studio Dash met with before his father's passing. Once our glasses are filled and we're all at the island, as we are often now, she says, "They want a decision right after the holiday and no later. It's a good deal, Dash. It will make you a richer man than you already are, not that you care about the money. The creative terms you wanted are almost all in place."

"I'll look it over," is all he says.

When Bella leaves, I take the opportunity to talk to him. "You still don't feel comfortable with that studio, do you?"

"I have a gut feeling they are going to butcher the project. They don't understand or care about my vision."

"Which is a mistake we've seen at the box office with many book-to-film projects, but maybe Bella got the wording right. Read it."

"After I finish the book. I'm close."

"Before Thanksgiving?"

"Probably after, but not by much."

I snap my fingers. "Well, get to work so I can read it."

He laughs and we end up on the living room floor, using the coffee table as our desks again.

I dig in my purse and eye Allison's journal, which I haven't touched in a week. I don't want to bother Dash with my worries for Allison right now and I text Neil: *Anything on the investigation?*

No, he says. *I'm good at my job and I haven't found her. That's not good for her.*

No, I think. It's not. I pull up Allison's number and type: *Where are you, Allison?*

No one replies.

CHAPTER FORTY-SEVEN

Thanksgiving turns into a memorable day. Dash and I wake up in bed together, drink coffee together, and end up in the shower together. We stand there holding each other with the water running over us and I don't miss the way he holds me a little tighter than usual. Both of his parents and his brother are gone. There's no way the holiday doesn't bring back memories of times when they were all a family. I'm worried about him today so I, too, hold him a little bit tighter than normal.

Once Bella arrives at the house, we head to my parents' place where Dash eases up a bit and is much more himself. Of course, my mother and stepfather greet us all with hugs and the house smells of divine temptations. Bella and my mother hit it off, and the three of us chat in the kitchen while finishing up the meal. Dash and my stepfather put up the tree and run the lights. We all stuff our faces, decorate the tree, and then watch Bella's father's race. I watch Dash, wondering if the father connection will rattle him, but he's wildly into the race, cheering, absorbed in the moment.

After her father wins said race, the group of us dig into the variety of desserts, of which, there are many. Bella finishes off a slice of coconut pie—my mother's coconut pie is to die for—and declares it, "The best thing I've ever eaten."

Dash agrees.

It's a good day, I think again, and Bella confirms as much as we leave my parents' house. "It was so nice to have a family holiday. Thank you for inviting me."

"Agreed," Dash chimes in. "A much-needed family holiday. The timing was appreciated."

My mother hugs him and I hear her whisper, "I hope there will be many more to follow." She eases back and says, "And I can't wait for your tree decorating party Saturday night."

We drop Bella off at her place and when Dash and I are alone, he says, "I needed that. More than you know." His voice is rough with emotion and he squeezes my hand.

I lean over and kiss his cheek. He captures my head and kisses me properly. "I want to spend every holiday with you. You know that, right?"

"Good," I whisper, emotions welling inside me. "Because I want to spend them with you as well."

When I settle back in my seat, I think about that word "forever", and decide that after all we have lived through together, it's easy to see that forever isn't always as long as we hope. It's critical we embrace every day we have in the life we are granted. And I plan to do so with Dash.

It's a long time later and Dash is working on his book while I look through the Christmas decorations Dash has dragged out of the closet for me, and I decide they're beautiful. One ornament, a snowflake star made of glass has me sucking in a breath. Dash sits down next to me and says, "You like it?"

"I do," I say. "It reminds me of an ornament my father gave me years ago. He didn't always send gifts, but when he did, I was a mix of angry and happy I can't really explain."

"I have a pretty good idea."

"Yes, I suppose you do. I want him to call me back and I don't know why."

"The same reason I wanted my father to call me. Our parents are a part of us."

"Yes. I know. You're right." I glance at the star and then back at him. "They say you can wish upon a star and have a wish granted."

"Isn't that a shooting star?"

"My mother always told me to pick a star, any star, and wish. What would Bella wish for?"

"Something for someone else. She's generous that way."

"Very true. And what would you wish for?"

"I already have my wish, Allie. You're here."

I warm with these words, with the feeling of being with that person my soul has always known was out there but somehow, I'd stopped believing. Until that necklace had arrived with my name on it—with *her* name on it. I shove aside the moment and touch Dash's cheek. "And I already have my wish. I'm here."

"Then I'd call us very lucky," he murmurs, stroking my hair behind my ear.

I shiver with his tender touch. "Then maybe we should wish for someone else," I challenge.

"I wish for Bella to find someone special. Now, your turn."

"I'm stingy with my wishes for other people," I declare. "I want Queen Compton and my mother to beat cancer forever. I too want Bella to find someone special as well. And—"

"*And?*" Dash prods.

My mind goes to the woman who inadvertently brought me to Dash, who changed my life. "I wish for Allison to come home safely."

CHAPTER FORTY-EIGHT

Dash calls Bella on Sunday night and accepts one of the TV and film offers he finally feels right about. An hour later, another studio wants to fly into Nashville for one last plea for Dash's rights. He agrees and a meeting is set for Tuesday night.

Monday comes first though, and that morning, Dash is eager to get our life back to normal. For us, that means I leave Dash at home working, deep into the final chapters of his book that I cannot wait to read. I stop by Tyler's office, but neither he nor his secretary are in right now. As the day ticks by, there is no sign of Tyler.

Tuesday morning, repeat. I leave Dash at home, sprinting to the finish line of his book, perhaps today. It's late afternoon when I manage a break from the chaos and stop by Tyler's office, but not only is he still not in, apparently his secretary is on vacation.

Once I'm back in my office, I just go for it and punch his number on my cellphone.

"Yes, Ms. Wright?" he answers on the first ring.

"Are you okay?"

He appears in my doorway. "Why would I *not* be okay?"

I set my phone down. "I haven't seen you. I haven't heard from you. Even your secretary is gone."

"I didn't know I was required to check-in with you."

"You're very arrogant, you know that?"

His lips curve. "Most women call that hard to get to know. It's mysterious and interesting."

My lips curve. I think he's joking. Then again, this is Tyler. Maybe he's serious. "I'm not most women."

"Yes, I'm exceedingly aware of that fact. How is Dash?"

"Good. Why don't you ask him yourself?" I say, and do so with the mindset of healing old wounds. Death has a way of showing you how easily "the end" can appear in life, how easily regret is created, and opportunities are missed. It's time to mend fences for everyone's good.

"I did," he surprises me by saying. "This morning when I stopped by your apartment," he adds. "I just thought you might offer a clearer picture of his mindset."

I blink in shock. "You went to see him today? Really? How did that go?"

"He invited me to the meeting with the studio. I know one of the main players quite well."

"That's good, right?"

"Yes, Allie. I do believe it is."

I hesitate, but I have to change the subject. I have asked the question he probably dreads from me. "Anything from Allison?"

His expression tightens. "Nothing. And I tried." He shuts down the topic, sideswipes me with a rapid topic change, or rather, command. "Send me an update on the auction."

"Already in your inbox."

He nods and disappears into the hallway. I stand up and shut my door before returning to my desk and dialing Dash. "Hey, baby," he answers.

"Hey. Anything I might want to know?"

"Tyler works fast," he says with a laugh. "He already told you."

"I might have encouraged him to make peace with you. You two were friends, Dash. And I really don't think—"

"We made peace, baby, the best we're going to without some time."

"You invited him to the meeting?"

"Yes. I think he's an asset and so does Bella. And for the record, I still think he'd fuck you if he got the chance, but the only way he gets that chance is if you let him and I know you won't. Now, I am about three chapters from done and haven't showered."

"Go finish. Dash, I love you."

"Show me tonight when we pop champagne and celebrate one of these deals." He softens his voice. "And I love you, too, baby."

We disconnect and I'm feeling hopeful about everything and everyone but Allison. I don't know what to do to help. Maybe there's nothing I can do, but isn't that what Dash said about him and his father? And that ended badly. I have to do something. I stand up and look around the office. This was her office. I found that plane ticket and never even brought that up to Neil. I quickly dig for it, shoot a photo, and text it to Neil. He replies with a phone call.

"Good work," he says when I answer. "I'll find out who else was on that flight. Have you searched the office well?"

"I—no, actually."

"Search when you get time. Or I can if you want to get me in after hours."

"I'll do a search right now. I'll let you know."

I start digging around, in files, on the bookshelf, and then finally in the credenza that I skimmed and saw nothing helpful. This time though, I find one hanging folder that is way in the back and blank. I grab it, and to my shock, find another journal. My heart leaps into my throat. I roll to the desk and open to page one:

This is nothing I thought I'd ever have to write, but I can't talk to anyone about this. When I met him, I was heartbroken, in love with a man who had rejected me.

Why I allowed myself to be seduced even slightly by this particular man, I do not know. It was wrong in every way and I knew it. He was married. I was never going to let it go too far. Ever. And I didn't. I didn't. I couldn't. But I did allow a flirtation, I know. I just—I needed to feel something other than pain. It felt good to have his interest. So when he asked me to drinks, I said yes. I know. I'm a horrible person. God, why did I go? Why? It hurts me to know I could hurt someone else, and as I said, he's married. Then things spiraled. They went badly. So very badly. I don't even know where to start. I can't seem to write it down. And I don't know how I keep going on.

My heart leaps. I'm terrified for Allison with what reads like someone suicidal.

I shoot a copy of the text and send it to Neil with a message: *Another journal. I'll copy it for you and scan it to email.*

That doesn't sound good, he replies. *Send it. I'm waiting on a contact to get me the flight info.*

An idea hits me and I type: *Should I send a company email and ask if anyone knows how to reach her?*

Not until I have the flight information and read that journal, he replies.

I'm worried, I text.

As am I, he confirms.

There's a knock on my door and I shut the journal and pull it to my lap. "Yes? Come in."

The door opens and to my shock, Jack is my visitor. "I have a very big client who just got into town. He wants to talk to you about a high-end family heirloom he wants to auction off. Can you join us for drinks?"

"When?"

"About thirty minutes."

"I—ah—yes. Of course."

"Good," he says, his intelligent eyes registering his approval. "See you soon." He disappears out into the hallway.

With no time for the copier, I start shooting photos of the entries, and upload them to a Dropbox folder. Once that is done, I send the link to Neil by text with a message that reads: *Meeting. I have to go. This was the best I can do and I've read nothing but a paragraph.*

Next, I text Dash: *Good Luck.*

He replies with: *Thanks, baby. See you soon.*

I text Bella the same: *Good luck. Knock 'em dead.*

Thanks, sweetie, she answers. *Love you.*

And I love her. I swear she's the sister I never had. One day I'll convince Dash to tell her everything about his brother. Once he's dared to tell us both everything, he'll know we both love him unconditionally, and he'll be closer to healing.

Setting that thought aside, for now, I quickly gather my things and walk to Katie's office, to find her behind her desk working. "I'm going to drinks with Jack and some client. Do you need anything?"

"I'm good. Wow, you've really filled Allison's shoes now. I told you she was up and coming here. She got Jack's attention as well."

"Yes, well, it's not well-timed, but it sounds like the client wants to work with Riptide and that will make my real boss in New York a happy man."

"Good luck," she says. "Text me and tell me about it."

"I will." I hurry down the hallway and find Jack at the elevator waiting on me.

"Ready?" he asks as the elevator door opens.

"I am," I say, and I step onto the car with Jack following.

LISA RENEE JONES

CHAPTER FORTY-NINE

Once we're in the elevator, Jack gives me a rather intimate inspection. "You look professional and pretty, Allie. I'm sure you'll get our client's attention."

Feeling awkward about the compliment I quickly reply in a professional tone, "I'm hoping it's the services Hawk Legal in partnership with Riptide can offer that gets their attention."

"Oh, we will," he says. "I have a feeling we're headed toward a beautiful partnership." The doors open at the lobby. "And it's okay to enjoy the compliment. It's human to enjoy being found pretty."

My awkwardness expands but I manage a pleasant, "Thank you," because I don't know what else to say, and since I want off this topic, I quickly step forward. Once we're in the garage elevator, I ask, "Who's the client we're meeting?"

"A big music producer named Nelson Miles. He's behind most of the top names in country music. The ones on our list, at least, and those are the ones that count." He winks.

That wink does not feel the way it does when Dash winks at me. It feels uncomfortable and I'm thankful the door opens. Jack holds the door for me since it has the rapid shut mechanism. I exit and he motions to a black Mercedes. He's a gentleman and opens my door for me, but I swear he looks at my legs as I slide them into the passenger area. I'm really regretting riding with him.

The car smells new and seems to have about every extra that can possibly be made. The seats are black leather, the heater warm, and the music playing a holiday tune. Once he joins me, he cranks the car, and pulls us outside the parking garage. The sun is beginning to set along Nashville's downtown skyline, and while I focus on it, Jack glances over at me. "I hear you decided to stay on with Riptide instead of Hawk Legal," he says, and suddenly I feel like I'm in a trap designed to change my mind.

"It's the best of both worlds."

"What do they do for you that we cannot?"

"I made some close connections there. Mrs. Compton, the founder of Riptide, is like a second mother."

"Do they pay you well?"

"Yes," I say. "Very well."

"Bonuses?"

"Yes," I confirm.

"How much will you get for this sale tonight if you close it?"

"A generous amount," I reply simply.

"What if I match it and add ten percent?"

"Your son already generously made that offer."

"My son isn't me."

No, I think. He's not. Jack has an easy confidence. Tyler's is more arrogant and reserved, but it's also more wounded, more human than I once thought. "No. But he's someone I've gotten to know well."

"How well?"

"Well enough to know he'll do right by me."

"As will I," he promises, glancing at the gas tank. "And we need gas." He turns into the gas station and pulls to the pump. "Give me a moment."

Feeling anxious, I try to occupy my mind, pulling up the photos I took for Neil and starting to read a random image toward the front of the journal. *He complimented me, made me feel beautiful. Made me feel that it was okay to need to feel beautiful. Don't we all need to feel beautiful? After being rejected, I was vulnerable, seeking validation. I think I was weak. I know I was weak. Had I just backed away from this, it never would have gone where it went.*

Did she actually let things get beyond flirtation? I got the impression she didn't, but now, I don't know. Was this an actual affair, I wonder? Or maybe she led him on a bit because he made her feel wanted? I just can't tell from the entries.

My gaze catches on a phone number scribbled in the lower corner of the page and I can't help myself, I dial it. At the same time, Jack's phone sitting just under the radio rings. Instinctively, I glance over it and go cold. It's my number. Jack was the man Allison was seeing. I'm cold and hot all over, my head spinning. My hand is trembling. I have no idea why, but I know I cannot let Jack know. I grab his phone to erase the call but of course, it's locked. I'm out of time. I don't know what to do. The door starts to open and I shove his phone under his seat, in the hopes he'll believe he dropped it. At least I bought myself time. We're three minutes from the meeting spot. Three minutes until I'm with him and other people. I'll figure out how to explain the call later.

And I'm not going to ride home with Jack.

CHAPTER FIFTY

Jack joins me again in a whiff of spicy, almost pungent cologne I haven't noticed until now. He smiles in my direction and cranks the engine. I can't muster a returned smile. In fact, I'm certain he can hear my heart racing, but if he does, he doesn't react. He also doesn't notice his missing phone. Once we arrive at the bar, I don't wait for him to open my door. I get out and meet him at the trunk. "When we're done here, let's hang back a moment and talk through your future with Hawk Legal."

"Actually, Dash has a big meeting tonight with a studio. I'm meeting him right after this to find out how that went."

"Right. You're seeing him. I remember that now."

He's playing coy. I know he's seen the press. "I'm living with him."

"Never settle for a diamond when you can have the stars and the sky." I have no idea what he's trying to say. Dash is a diamond and Jack is the stars and the sky? Whatever the point, he motions me toward the door. "Let's go knock 'em dead, tiger."

Anything to get me inside, with other people, and not just him.

I follow his lead and enter the bar, only to have the record producer waiting on us, with an entourage of three more. We're quickly ushered to a table and thankfully, I end up sitting far from Jack. I'm drawn into conversation and it's all I can do to focus. Nelson is tall, dresses like a cowboy, and talks with a southern charm I can relate to easily. He's one of my people, as us southerners say, and we connect. The family heirloom is just that to a music guy, I guess. His dad worked for the Beatles when they toured and he has a treasure trove of Beatles collectibles. Mark will be pleased, as will Queen Compton when she's back to work.

When everyone orders another round, Jack begins searching for his phone. When he excuses himself to go to his car, I know I need to leave. I've already thought this through. I order an Uber, which is only three minutes away. I glance at Nelson. "I have another meeting. I need to leave. Jack knows about it. I'm going to run." I glance at my phone. "I have a car on its way."

"Well, it's been mighty nice to meet you, pretty lady. I hope we can make this work."

"I'll call you tomorrow," I promise and stand up, saying a quick goodbye to everyone.

I hurry to the bathroom and exit the side door. My car is about to pull to the front door. I call the driver. "I'm at the back door."

"You got it," the woman says.

Jack exits the restaurant. He's found me. "Allie? What's going on?"

Come on, Uber. "I tried to call you," I say, just hoping he doesn't look at the time stamp. "Dash is done with his meeting. There's something big going on. I have to find out what."

"So you're leaving a client meeting early?"

"They're sold, Jack."

The car pulls up and I flag the driver. When she pulls right next to me, I open the door. "I'll come see you in the morning."

"How'd you get my number, Allie?"

"I grabbed it from Allison's work logs," I say, desperately trying to lie myself out of this, when lies rarely save anyone. "I hope that doesn't bother you? I guess I should have asked if I could use it. I really have to go."

"All right. Yes. Come see me, Allie."

I nod and climb into the car, shutting the door, and breathing out. My hands are clammy. I was scared, I realize. I was scared of Jack.

Once the car is moving, I text Neil, *Allison had a phone number in the journal. It belongs to Jack Hawk. Anything connecting them?*"

He calls me. "Yes," he says, as I answer. "They had quite a lot of communication. I haven't heard back from my guy on the plane manifest, but since her journals reflect an affair with an older man, I'm guessing it was him."

"Me, too."

"And how did you figure this out?"

"I stupidly called the number she wrote down and it was his phone. I was with him for a drink meeting with clients. It's a long story, but I'm in an Uber headed home."

"Good. I don't feel right about this Jack thing. Oh. There is what looks like a combination to a lock in the notes she had scribbled on a back page."

My mind goes to Tyler's grandmother's house. "There was a safe downstairs in the house I was staying in, the one where Allison stayed, too.

"Can you meet me at the house?"

"Yes, I can."

"Good. I have a feeling about this. I'll meet you there. I'm about twenty minutes out."

"I'm five. Hold on." I lean forward and give the Uber driver the address with the promise of a big tip. "Okay, I'm headed there. I can't be sure I can get in and I can't call Tyler. Jack is his father, and while they aren't close,

I just—I don't feel good about it. And he's in a meeting anyway."

"Where is Dash?"

"The same meeting Tyler is at. A big Hollywood meeting. We can't disturb him."

"All right. If you can't get into the house, I can. Stay in the Uber until I get there."

CHAPTER FIFTY-ONE

The house is dark, empty, and kind of creepy looking tonight.

"This is it," the woman announces.

"Can I pay you to wait until my friend arrives?"

"Honey, I'm sorry. My son has a choir program in twenty minutes. I can't miss it. You were my last pickup. As it is, I'm pushing it."

Great. Dash is going to kill me for going in there alone, but what can I do at this point?

"I understand." I hand her cash for the extra ride and the tip, and exit the car. Hurrying forward, the exterior of the house is dark, and I pray that the code still works, but I'm not optimistic.

Using the flashlight on my phone, eager to seek shelter, I shine the light on my path and then the door panel. To my relief, the door opens. I hurry inside, turn on the lights and then text Neil: *My driver had to go but I'm inside.*

Damn it, he replies. *I told you to wait. I'm still fifteen minutes out.*

Give me the code, I answer. *Let me get in the safe so we can get out of here. And hurry, please. It feels creepy in here.*

He sends me a combination with another "damn it" attached. I lock the door. He can knock. I need to be safe. After that, I hurry to the cellar door and draw a breath. I'll be fine. I'm safe. Neil is on his way. I flip on the light, rush down the stairs and go down on my knees in front of the safe. I use the code and it opens. There are two sealed envelopes. One is addressed to the police and one is addressed to Mary Hawk, Jack's wife. My stomach knots with the certainty that this is going no place good. With a trembling hand, I quickly open the letter to the police and start reading:

It reads "copy" on the front.

Dear Mary,

It is my greatest heartache to do this to you. I know you've been married a very long time. I know you must love your husband. The problem is that he's not the man you think he is. I was dating your son. I love your son, but he broke up with me, and Jack, well he offered me comfort. He looks like Tyler and he has some of the same traits. I was drawn to him, but not romantically. Fatherly. I was holding onto a connection to Tyler. And then—then he tried—I can barely write it. He cornered me. He ripped my shirt. He touched me inappropriately. It was at the office and a cleaning crew interrupted. They saved me. I know the crew saw what happened. They knew I was crying. I resigned the next day. I didn't tell Tyler. I was ashamed. I love him too much to take his father from him, but Jack was— violent. I don't want you to get hurt. I don't want someone else to get hurt. Please protect yourself. My deepest apologies.

"You really do look like her."

At the sound of Jack's voice, I quake inside. Somehow, I think to shove the letters in the safe, and shut it before I stand to face him. His tie is loose, his jacket disheveled. "What are you doing here, Jack? And how did you even get in here?"

"I'm Tyler's father. You think I don't have the passcode for his grandmother's house, my *mother's* house?"

"Okay. Then *why* are you here?" I repeat, my nerves on edge, everything about me trapped in a cellar with this man is spelling trouble.

WHEN I SAY YES

"You know why I'm here, Allie. We both know why I'm here."

For no good reason, I think, trying to buy time for Neil to get here. "You left your clients to follow me?"

"I take the safety of those in my care seriously." He closes the space between us and I back up, but there is nowhere to go. I hit the safe. And the next thing I know, he's grabbing me, his hand wrapped around my hair. "Stop. Let me go." I shove against his unmoving body.

He jerks my hair harder, pain ripping through my scalp, forcing me to still. "This isn't your game, Allie. It was hers and neither of you should have tested me. Now someone is going to come here and take you away, just like they did her. And it didn't have to be that way."

Adrenaline courses through me and I no longer care about the pain. Someone is coming to get me and no one will ever see me again. I shove at him, but he catches my hands, his leg capturing my leg. And then his mouth is on my mouth. *Oh no. No. No.* I bite him. Hard. "Bitch. What the fuck are you doing? Ask to be saved. Give me a reason to save you."

"Let me go. You're the one who needs to be saved."

He laughs and turns me, shoving me to my knees, and not gently. "Open the safe."

"No."

"Open the fucking safe. I want those letters."

Now I know it was him in the house that night, looking for what she must have told him existed.

"Open it and I'll let you go. Refuse and I won't just end you tonight. I'll end your mother."

Kill. He means kill my mother. Fear quakes inside me for her, not me. Because I believe him. He killed Allison. He will kill me and my mother. I open the damn safe. He reaches around me and grabs the letters. Then to my horror, he bends me over the safe, and yanks up my skirt. I scream, I scream with all that I have in me, and suddenly he's gone. I yank at my skirt, pull it down as I turn to find Jack on the floor, bleeding out, and an unfamiliar man holding a gun, which must have a silencer, standing on the opposite side of the body, facing me.

He's tall, muscular, with hard features, and dark hair slashes with gray at his temples. He's in jeans, a T-shirt, and a leather jacket. He looks like anyone you might see on the street except that he's not.

"Ghost," I say and it's not a question. I know who he is from Dash's description of the brutal assassin.

"Yes, sweetheart." He shoves the gun in a holster under his jacket. "At your service. I couldn't let that dick fuck you or kill you. Dash would never write another damn word."

"You," I swallow hard, and try again, "you kill people, but you saved my life." It's a statement of fact, and a question. I'm in a twilight zone and have no idea what is going on. Not really. This cannot be my life.

He shrugs. "I kill people I want to kill. I don't want to kill you."

I hug myself, dampness clinging to my cheeks. "How did you know to come here?"

"I saw that interview he did where he proclaimed you his goddess and all that shit."

"He didn't—"

"Close enough. I came to meet you. I figured you'd fuck everything up for me and Dash and maybe you needed to die."

"Oh," I whisper. "You're here to kill me?"

"Hell no. He's so fucking into you. If you die, that'll fuck him up even worse. I decided you need to live."

"So, you're not—Jack said he called someone to—"

"Kill you. He did. I'm above his paygrade. He's rich, but not rich enough to pay me what I'm worth. He called another guy, I'll handle him. You have nothing to worry about."

"My God." I press my hand to my forehead. "He really was going to have me killed."

"Yeah, but I saved you." He flexes. "Your hero."

"Did he have Allison killed?" The question trembles from my mouth, and I hold my breath, afraid of the answer I already know he'll give me. I just need confirmation.

"Yeah." He says matter-of-factly. "She's gone. Same guy who was coming for you. He's nowhere near as good a killer as me, but he's good. They'll never find her."

"Can you find out where she is?"

"I can't get him to talk, but I can kill him. You want me to kill him? It'll be a favor. On the house and all that."

"No. I mean—will he kill me?"

"Not and get a payday, and he likes money. But you know what, he was going to kill you. I'm going to kill him. I want to." He glances at what I believe to be a Rolex and then eyes me. "I better fly this joint. Tell the police the truth, but leave me out of it. He was attacking you. Someone shot him from behind. He died. You didn't see who did it. I killed the cameras, and the forensics will match up." He starts to turn and shifts back to me. "You're not going to keep him from writing, are you?"

"No," I say quickly. "I was an editor. I love his books. I love how he writes you."

"Has he written the new book?"

"He just finished."

"Have you read it?"

"Part of it. You're gonna love it."

"Hmm. We'll see. You know, I've decided I like the idea of you. Tell him to write me a woman, someone like you, all soft and sweet, but somehow tough enough to handle my shit. He'll figure it out." He points at me. "Stay out of trouble, Allie. I might not be here to save you next time and then we're all fucked." He turns and runs up the stairs.

I watch him leave and then my gaze goes to the hole in the back of Jack's head, the blood pouring out onto the floor and I start to tremble all over. I can't stop trembling and tears are streaming down my face. Suddenly, Dash is there, cupping my face, kissing me, and then scooping me up and carrying me up the stairs.

CHAPTER FIFTY-TWO

I snuggle into Dash's chest and shut my eyes, blocking out everything but him rescuing me, him walking with me in his arms. I don't know what happens, though. I'm suddenly on my feet and Dash's voice is breaking through the white noise.

"Allie. Allie, are you okay?"

"How are you here?" I ask, trying to get a grip on reality.

"Ghost called me."

"He saved my life." I grab his wrist, where his hand still touches my face, trying to stabilize myself as memories crash into me—Jack, Ghost, the letters Allison wrote to the police, and to Mary. "Dash, he saved my life."

"What scares the shit out of me is how damn easily he could have taken it."

"Jack called someone to kill me. Ghost killed Jack and he's killing that someone because he took the job. For you. He saved me for you."

All of a sudden, police and EMS swarm us and my head is spinning. I'm aware of the medical staff checking my vitals and I'm just present enough to be pretty sure I'm in shock. As if reading my mind, the EMS tech, a man with dark hair, says, "You're experiencing shock. I'm going to give you a sedative."

I grab his hand. "No. I have to be able to tell people what happened. I need to tell people—" I look around in desperation. "Dash?"

"I'm here, baby," he says, and only then do I even realize that I'm on a chair and he's on his knees in front of me.

"I need to talk to you," I say. "I need to talk to you now."

He glances at the EMS tech. "Give us a minute."

"I need to ensure she's stable," the tech says. "And then the police want to talk to her."

"*Give us a minute*," Dash says, his tone sharp.

The man gives a quick nod and backs away. The minute I'm alone with Dash again, if you can call being surrounded by emergency crews alone, I say, "Jack was going to have me killed," I say and oddly as I say the words, I start to come back to me again, to what happened. "He called for someone, someone like Ghost to kill me. But Ghost said he's handling it. And there are letters in the safe from Allison. He tried to rape her and she was going to expose him. He was on top of me trying to rape me when—when Ghost shot him."

"If he hadn't killed him, I would have, but you can't mention him to the police. He can find us, but no one can ever find him. He's a better friend than enemy."

"Yes. Yes, but even as a friend he scares me."

"One day he'll let down his guard and it will be the end of him, but today isn't that day. Okay?"

"Yes. Yes, okay. We have to call Tyler. She's dead. Allison is dead and so is his father."

"And we will. Can you talk to the police and get this over with so I can take you home?"

"Yes." A thought hits me. "Neil. Is he okay?"

"Pissed at you for coming inside without him, but yes, he's fine. He got here after me. He's locked out of the crime scene. Let's get the police over with."

I nod. "Yes. Please."

Dash stands and motions to a man in plain clothes. He joins us, asks me a few questions, and the minute he hears exactly what happened, he motions to a female detective. Karen is petite, brunette, and pretty with a delicate way about her, which includes taking me to a police car where we both sit in the back seat and talk. It's a long time later when that talk ends and I'm free to go.

I exit the car and Dash is immediately there pulling me close. "How did it go?"

"I told her I didn't see the shooter. She said Jack had a lot of enemies. It almost sounded like he was already on their radar. I can go home, but they're going to come by to talk to me again tomorrow, and pick up the necklace. I have to call my mother."

"I already did. She's going to come over tomorrow."

Bella joins us, wrapping me in a bear hug. "My God, woman, you scared me to death. Don't do that ever again."

"How'd you even get behind the tape?" I ask.

"I came with Dash. I was already here. I'm so sorry this happened to you. Are you okay?"

We chat for a minute or two when my gaze lands on Tyler, just outside the yellow tape, and in conversation with a police officer. Dash and Bella follow my gaze and Bella says, "This is going to be hell for him."

Tyler shows his ID to the officer and then he's allowed to cross the tape. Dash glances at me. "Stay here, baby," he says, and then he's walking toward Tyler.

Bella and I watch the two men speak for a moment, and I assume Dash has given him all the horrible news, when Tyler's chin lowers, his shoulders sinking forward. Dash's hand is on Tyler's arm, a show of comfort that ends when a detective approaches them. Bella and I don't speak. We just watch it all happen. The conversation with Dash, the detective, and Tyler continues for a minute or two before Tyler breaks from Dash and heads back toward the police lineup.

Bella and I rush toward Dash. "What just happened?" Bella asks before I can.

"The detective is going to Tyler's house," Dash explains. "Tyler is not exactly feeling himself right now."

"I'm going with him," Bella says. "He can't be alone."

Dash catches her arm. "Bella—"

"I can handle this, Dash. He needs someone."

"Be careful with Tyler."

"I will," she promises. "I will, but I've known him for years and he is our friend, no matter what has gone down between you two. I need to go." She pulls away from Dash and rushes after Tyler.

"She's going to end up in bed with him," Dash says. "He's going to hurt her."

"Or maybe she'll save him."

He glances down at me. "I like your version of how this ends better than mine. Let's go home, baby."

CHAPTER FIFTY-THREE

The minute Dash and I walk into our apartment, Dash locks the door and scoops me up. "I can walk," I assure him.

"But you don't have to," he says, heading toward the bedroom, my hero, whisking me away to safety, or in this case our bathroom, where he lowers me to my feet beside the tub.

"Sit," he orders as I claim the ledge around the tub with my backside and he plugs the tub and starts the water. Almost as if he knows just how much I need to wash the dirt of this night off of me.

"Thank you, Dash."

His hands come down on my face and he tilts my gaze to his. "I'm going to get you a glass of wine to calm your nerves."

"Yes. Yes, that sounds good."

He strokes my cheek with a tender touch and leaves me sitting there on the edge of the tub. I know I should get up and undress, but I find myself reading that letter again in my mind. Jack used his friendliness combined with his power as a way to slide under people's radar. He was a predator, but just thinking of him lying there dead and bleeding, that damn hole in his head, is just too much. Tyler's words run through my mind: "The illusion of having what we do not."

Sometimes that illusion is another day of living with the people we love. So easily, that illusion could have been mine.

I blink and Dash is back in front of me, kneeling in front of me. "You okay?"

"Yes." I press my hand to his face. "Because of you, Dash. Ghost didn't save me. You did that from the day I met you." I laugh, but it's a bit of a choked sound. "He told me to tell you to write him a woman. One who is—"

"Like you?"

"Gentle but tough enough to handle him," I say, "or something like that."

"Like you," he says. "I guess he and I have that in common. You're the dream woman."

I laugh. "I don't know about that."

"I do. Allie, I was going to wait until Christmas Day to do this, but I can't wait. I can't think of another day of my life without you."

"Well, let's hope you don't have to. I think I have a personal bodyguard."

"Me," he says. "Allie, marry me."

I blink. "What?"

"Marry me. I cannot be without you."

"Dash," I say, tears welling in my eyes. "You don't have to do this, and don't do this tonight when you're affected by what happened."

"This isn't about tonight." He reaches into his pocket, producing a stunning circle diamond that glistens in the light. "I already planned to propose, baby. I love you and I feel like I almost lost you tonight. I just—I needed to do it now."

Tears escape down my cheeks. "Oh my God." The tears become real crying, an explosion of emotion.

Dash pushes to his feet and folds me close, his hand pressed between my shoulder blades. "I'm sorry." He strokes hair from my face. "I'm so sorry, Allie. This was horrible timing. I just thought—"

"Yes," I whisper. "Yes, I will marry you and no, it's not bad timing. It's perfect timing because that man—he made me feel—and you make me feel—yes," I say again.

"Are you sure?"

"Oh my God, Dash. Are you serious? Of course, I'm sure."

"Then why are you crying?" he asks, wiping the tears from my cheek.

"Happy tears and just emotional overload. I need to sit."

He eases his hold on me and I sit back down. He goes down on his knee again in front of me. "You want to put the ring on?"

"Yes. Of course, I do. It's gorgeous." I hold out my hand and Dash slides the ring on my finger. "I love it so much," I say, looking down at him. "And I love you." I wrap my arms around his neck. "Now get me naked and make me forget that man's hands on my body."

"Allie," he says softly, tenderly.

"I'm serious." I stand and he stands with me. "Make me forget." I tug on his shirt.

He pulls it over his head, and then leans around me, turning off the water. The next thing I know, he's scooped me up again, and this time he carries me to bed. Dash undresses me slowly, kissing me tenderly everywhere. And when we are naked and he's inside me, we make love. I am lost in him and everything else fades away.

LISA RENEE JONES

CHAPTER FIFTY-FOUR

The next day, I wake with Dash wrapped around me from behind, the warmth of his body and a ring on my finger. I stare at the stunning stone, thinking about the proposal rather than the horrible events of the night before.

"What are you thinking?" Dash asks, nuzzling my neck, and letting me know he's awake.

"How much I love it and you," I say, and just that easily, passion consumes us.

It's a long time later when we shower and dress, and just in time. The doorbell rings and my mother and stepfather are here. Of course, my mother is freaked out, but the minute she sees my ring, worry shifts to happiness. "This calls for a celebratory breakfast," she declares and then takes over our kitchen.

Bella, of course, calls me and Dash to check on us, but she's still with Tyler. I think Dash is right. She is becoming involved with Tyler, which worries me only because he's a damaged man, more damaged now by the pain of betrayal and loss. But things happen for a reason. Maybe, just maybe, they are meant to come together.

Karen, the detective from last night, shows up in the late afternoon, and picks up the necklace, asking only a few more questions. I'm sure more will follow, but for now, I have a break.

Later that evening, Bella comes over, brings dinner, and raves about my ring. We have a moment alone and I seize it. "You and Tyler?"

"I don't know what this is," she says. "I saw him hurting and I just needed to be there for him. That's all."

"Are you sure you're not setting yourself up for trouble? He's hurting, rebounding, and grieving, all at the same time."

"I know he's in a bad place. I know getting close to him now is risky, but I'm not turning my back on him. Besides, we've always been friends."

There is a part of me that can't see Tyler right now as anyone but Jack's son, but she can. And maybe that is exactly how she saves him. When she leaves, I walk to the star on the tree and make a wish for her and for Tyler to just be safe and happy.

***

Against Dash's wishes, I go back to work on Monday, aware that stability is needed by those in the office.

I'm shocked to discover Tyler has returned as well. I intend to go check on him, but he finds me first, stepping into my office and shutting the door. "I'm sorry for what happened to you, Allie."

I stand and round my desk to stop in front of him. "I'm sorry for what happened to you and her." I can't bring myself to bring up Jack. "I gave her journals to the police, but I have copies if you decide you want them."

"I'm not ready," he says.

"I know. She loved you intensely. Just know that."

"And I pushed her away and right into his trap."

"What happened to Allison wasn't your fault. Jack did this, not you."

"Right," he says and when he starts to turn, I throw myself at him and hug him.

He's stiff for a moment, but then he hugs me back. When I ease away from him, staring up at him, his eyes are bloodshot, pain radiating off of him. I want to say more, I want to help him but he shuts me down. "Get to work, Ms. Wright."

I smile through my teary eyes and say, "I'll be right here."

"Good," he says, simply, and to me, that's his way of saying "thank you" and that I'm valued.

He starts to turn and then says, "Her cat was at the shelter where she volunteered. I found her on their website. They had no idea it was her cat. I called and adopted her." With that, he turns and leaves, and my heart squeezes. He has her cat. My God, he really loved her. I hunt for the tissue box.

***

Christmas arrives quickly and while Dash, Bella, and I enjoy a family meal with my mom and stepdad, Tyler is with his mother, who has left him in charge of the company. Dash and I exchange gifts with everyone at the house but save ours for at home. We have just left my parent's place when my cellphone rings with my father's number. I glance over at Dash. "You going to answer it?"

I nod and take the call. "Merry Christmas, Allie."

"Merry Christmas," I say, a twist in my gut.

"I've been out of the country. I lost my phone and for the life of them, the cellphone company couldn't get my number on a new phone over there. I just got back and got it fixed. Not only did I see your calls, I was told you came by my apartment."

"I did," I say. "I thought you called. Or texted. But I think I was confused on that."

"No, but not because I didn't want to. You made it clear I wasn't welcomed in your life." He hesitates. "I didn't know that crap Brandon pulled."

"Why didn't you say that?"

"You were quick to believe me guilty and hell, why wouldn't you? I haven't been the best father."

"I should have given you the chance to speak on the matter. I was wrong. I'm sorry."

"Not as sorry as I am. How is your mother? Did she beat cancer?"

"She did."

"Good. She won't believe this, but she really was the love of my life. I took her for granted. Youth and money can do that to a man. Speaking of, I hear you're dating Dash Black."

"I am," I say. "He's a good man."

"Maybe one day you'll think I am, too, and I can meet him. Go enjoy Christmas. I'm on air this evening, so I have to get to the studio. When you're ready, say the word, and I'll come visit you."

"I think I'd like that."

"Good. I hope so."

We disconnect and I glance over at Dash. "He says he didn't know about Brandon."

"Do you believe him?"

"I want to. He wants to come visit and meet you, too. I just don't want to get hurt again."

"You've been through a lot this past few weeks. Maybe in the new year, you'll feel ready."

"Yes. Maybe I will. What is that saying, *life is short and it's here to be lived*?"

"Yes," he agrees. "That's the saying. I don't know who said it, but it feels like words to embrace."

***

Once we're home, Dash insists he give me my gift first. To my surprise, he blindfolds me and actually leads me out of the apartment. "Where are we going?" I ask, laughing as I realize we're in the elevator.

"First stop: the parking garage," he says, nuzzling my neck and tickling my ear with his hair. I'm laughing all over again when we step off the car into the garage.

"Now what?" I ask, smiling with the anticipation of what comes next.

Dash pulls off my blindfold, and I find a silver Beamer with a huge bow on it right in front of me.

"Oh my God, Dash." I glance over at him. "Are you serious? It's so expensive. And you already got me a ring."

He holds up the key. "Want to drive it?"

"Yes," I say, bubbling with excitement.

We climb into the car and I run my hand over the leather. "It's so pretty and it smells new."

"Driver her, baby."

"I think I will," I agree, cranking the engine.

We drive around the block. "I can't wait to show my mother," I say when we park and return to the apartment.

"I'm sure she'll be right over," he says as we settle onto the couch.

"Yes. Yes, she will. I better call her tomorrow."

"Now it's your turn," I say, handing him my gift in a velvet box with a red bow, that's not nearly as big as the one on the car.

His brows knit and he opens the box to display a black tungsten ring with diamonds around it.

"Look at the inscription," I say, and Dash reads it out loud, "You save me every day."

Dash looks at me with love in his eyes and slides the ring on before pulling me close. "And you, Allie, save me every day."

***

The night of the auction, it snows, just tiny flutters that fade in the wind, but even that is a near miracle in Nashville in December. It feels as if Allison is here, blessing the good work we are trying to do. And we do exactly that: good work. The auction is wildly successful.

I stand in the event room in a silver gown I picked out for the occasion, with Dash looking brutally handsome in a tuxedo, and watch the final item close with elation in my heart.

A fan steps to Dash's side and starts talking to him while Benjamin steps to my side. "Hi, Allie."

"Hi," I say, turning to face him. "How are you, Benjamin?"

"I wanted to apologize to you."

I frown. "For what?"

"I knew Jack was a pervert. That's why I said I wasn't surprised when Allison left. He showed her too much attention. I should have warned you."

"Thank you for saying that, but please don't blame yourself."

He shocks me by hugging me and then walking away. Dash steps to my side, "What was that?"

"It appears more people knew what Jack was like than I realized. He apologized for not warning me about him."

Later that night, Dash and I open a bottle of expensive champagne as he finally signs a contract for both a television show and a movie deal. "Ghost will be happy," I say.

"Even happier when he realizes I wrote in a woman for him in the next book."

"You rewrote the book for him?"

"I wrote it before he even asked. I was inspired." He drags me across his lap and cups my head. "By you, my little cupcake."

WHEN I SAY YES

I laugh and he kisses me, and this editor who'd soured on happily ever after stories, now believes in them once again.

EPILOGUE

On New Year's Eve, Dash and I stay home, drink champagne, and watch the explosion of Nashville's city lights below us. Bella, on the other hand, is with Tyler, which doesn't please Dash, but he's come to terms with the fact that he doesn't control her life.

"Let's talk about a wedding date and place," Dash says, refilling my glass.

"How about here?"

"How about we buy a house on the outskirts of Nashville, something we pick together, and we can have it there?"

"And give up the apartment?"

"No, I say let's keep it."

"I like that. Can we have horses?" I ask, starting to get excited.

"We can," he says. "Do you ride?"

"No. Do you?"

"A little. We'll learn."

"What about a dog?"

"We travel a lot."

"Henry Cavil travels with his dog. He posts pictures on Instagram of his giant dog traveling with him all the time."

He laughs. "If Henry Cavil does it, we can, too."

I grin, and remember Queen Compton's words, changing them just slightly to fit the moment. "Yes, we can. And then you can give Ghost a dog."

He chuckles. "I don't know about that one. What about a wedding date?"

"Next Christmas? No. The auction would need to move to a different date. It's too close to the holidays.

What about fall, when the leaves will be turning? Surely if we buy a house outside the city, it will be a perfect time of year. October?"

"I like it," he says. "October it is. I'll call a realtor next week."

It's almost midnight and Dash motions to my glass. "Let's countdown."

And so, we do. We countdown and then we kiss in the first moment of the year we will become Mr. and Mrs. Dash Black.

***

It's late January and I've managed to work out all the details to work for Riptide as a contractor for Hawk Legal. I also work from home as I please, which is about half-time. Bella has continued to see Tyler, and under her influence, he's softened, become even more human.

One Friday evening, Tyler appears in my doorway. "I'm ready."

I don't have to ask for what. He means the journals. "I'll send you a Dropbox link."

"I'm going to hold a memorial service for her. I thought maybe I'd pick a few words in her own voice to read. Maybe you can help me pick something out that isn't about me being an asshole."

"I'd be honored."

He gives me a small nod and disappears into the hallway, but I swear I can still feel his heart bleeding for Allison.

She's gone, but she is not forgotten.

***

Being shut out of his father's memorial is rough on Dash. The idea that his father's and his stepmother's hatred for him would dictate the absence of a proper funeral is also hard for him to accept. But in darkness, there is always light and we decide to embrace that light. On the day of his father's memorial, a private event, not open to the public, Dash and I hold our own celebration of his life. We sit in our bedroom seating area by the window, with the fireplace on, drinking his dad's favorite brandy coffee, and we read his last book to each other. Dash cries that day. It's the first time, even since his father passed, that I've seen him cry. It feels like progress, like he's allowing himself to be human. It's one step closer to him healing. And if it's the last thing I do in this lifetime, I will see the day he forgives himself. And I will love him more than he can love himself.

THE END

Don't forget, if you want to be the first to know about upcoming books, giveaways, sales, and any other exciting news I have to share please be sure you're signed up for my newsletter! As an added bonus everyone receives a free eBook when they sign-up!

http://lisareneejones.com/newsletter-sign-up/

***

Don't miss the Lucifer Trilogy coming soon—the latest Walker Security series!

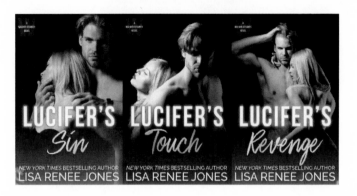

Tall, dark, and deadly, these men run Walker Security. Each is unique in his methods and skills, but all share key similarities. They are passionate about those they love, relentless when fighting for a cause they believe in, and all believe that no case is too hard, no danger too dark. Dedication is what they deliver, results are their reward.

Meet Lucifer, one of those men...

A man with demons that run deep and dark...

The only woman who can bring him to his knees...

As one of the newest members of Walker Security, Lucifer lives up to his name. He's a man with demons that run deep and dark. A man with secrets. A man betrayed by a woman, and that betrayal has shaped every part of his life moving forward.

He lives on the edge with fast cars, faster women, and some might say a death wish. That is until he crossed paths with Walker Security and one of their own pulled him from the bowels of his self-created hell.

But his own personal devil is about to show herself again. That woman from his past is back, and nothing is as it seems.

https://www.lisareneejones.com/walker-security-lucifers-trilogy.html

***

And don't miss the next book in the Lilah Love series—
HAPPY DEATH DAY!

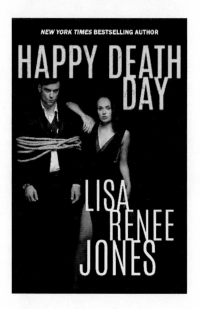

Kane Mendez.

The son of a drug lord, who is not his father's son, and yet, he has enemies. Too many enemies.

Lilah Love.

The FBI agent who perhaps kills a little too easily. Or does she? As she's called in to consult on a case, and catch a killer, her troubles back home don't go away. People want her dead. She simply wants them dead first.

Kane and Lilah. Lilah and Kane. War is on the horizon. And everyone won't survive.

https://www.lisareneejonesthrillers.com/the-lilah-love-series.html#HappyDeathDay

BE THE FIRST TO KNOW!

The best way to be informed of all upcoming books, sales, giveaways, and to get a FREE EBOOK, be sure you're signed up for my newsletter list!

SIGN-UP HERE: http://lisareneejones.com/newsletter-sign-up/

Another surefire way to be in the know is to follow me on social media:

Facebook: https://www.facebook.com/AuthorLisaReneeJones/
Facebook Group: https://www.facebook.com/groups/LRJbooks
Instagram: https://www.instagram.com/lisareneejones/
TikTok: https://www.tiktok.com/@lisareneejonesbooks
Twitter: http://www.twitter.com/LisaReneeJones
BookBub: https://www.bookbub.com/authors/lisa-renee-jones

EXCERPT FROM THE WALKER SECURITY: ADRIAN TRILOGY

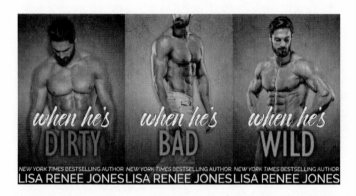

I exit the bathroom and halt to find him standing in the doorway, his hands on either side of the doorframe. "What are you doing?

"This," he says, and suddenly, his hands are on my waist, and he's walked me back into the bathroom.

Before I know what's happening, he's kicked the door shut, and his fingers are diving into my hair. "Kissing you, because I can't fucking help myself. And because you might not ever let me do it again. That is unless you object?"

That's the part that really gets me. The "unless I object," the way he manages to be all alpha and demanding and still ask. Well, and the part where he can't fucking help himself.

I press to my toes and the minute my mouth meets his, his crashes over mine, his tongue doing a wicked lick that I feel in every part of me. And I don't know what I taste like to him, but he is temptation with a hint of tequila, demand, and desire. His hands slide up my back, fingers splayed between my shoulder blades, his hard body pressed to mine, seducing me in every possible way.

I moan with the feel of him and his lips part from mine, lingering there a moment before he says, "Obviously, someone needs to protect you from me," he says. "Like me." And then to my shock, he releases me and leaves. The bathroom door is open and closed before I know what's happened. And once again, I have no idea if or when I will ever see him again.

FIND OUT MORE ABOUT THE ADRIAN TRILOGY HERE:

https://www.lisareneejones.com/walker-security-adrians-trilogy.html

GET A FREE COPY OF BOOK ONE HERE:

https://claims.prolificworks.com/free/I3n4VacJ

THE BRILLIANCE TRILOGY

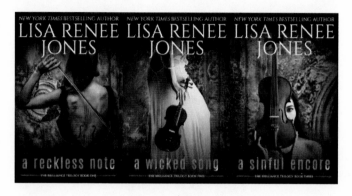

It all started with a note, just a simple note handwritten by a woman I didn't know, never even met. But in that note is perhaps every answer to every question I've ever had in my life. And because of that note, I look for her but find him. I'm drawn to his passion, his talent, a darkness in him that somehow becomes my light, my life. Kace August is rich, powerful, a rock star of violins, a man who is all tattoos, leather, good looks, and talent. He has a wickedly sweet ability to play the violin, seducing audiences worldwide. Now, he's seducing me. I know he has secrets. I don't care. Because you see, I have secrets, too.

I'm not Aria Alard, as he believes. I'm Aria Stradivari, daughter to Alessandro Stradivari, a musician born from the same blood as the man who created the famous Stradivarius violin. I am as rare as the mere 650 instruments my ancestors created. Instruments worth millions. 650 masterpieces, the brilliance unmatched. 650 reasons to kill. 650 reasons to hide. One reason not to: him.

FIND OUT MORE ABOUT THE BRILLIANCE TRILOGY HERE:

https://www.lisareneejones.com/brilliance-trilogy.html

GET A FREE COPY OF BOOK ONE HERE:

https://claims.prolificworks.com/free/FTpzSTRe

ALSO BY LISA RENEE JONES

THE INSIDE OUT SERIES

If I Were You
Being Me
Revealing Us
His Secrets*
Rebecca's Lost Journals
The Master Undone*
My Hunger*
No In Between
My Control*
I Belong to You
All of Me*

THE SECRET LIFE OF AMY BENSEN

Escaping Reality
Infinite Possibilities
Forsaken
Unbroken*

CARELESS WHISPERS

Denial
Demand
Surrender

WHITE LIES

Provocative
Shameless

TALL, DARK & DEADLY

Hot Secrets
Dangerous Secrets
Beneath the Secrets

WALKER SECURITY

Deep Under
Pulled Under
Falling Under

LILAH LOVE

Murder Notes
Murder Girl
Love Me Dead
Love Kills
Bloody Vows
Bloody Love
Happy Death Day
The Party's Over

DIRTY RICH

Dirty Rich One Night Stand
Dirty Rich Cinderella Story
Dirty Rich Obsession
Dirty Rich Betrayal
Dirty Rich Cinderella Story: Ever After
Dirty Rich One Night Stand: Two Years Later
Dirty Rich Obsession: All Mine
Dirty Rich Secrets
Dirty Rich Betrayal: Love Me Forever

THE FILTHY TRILOGY

266

WHEN I SAY YES

The Bastard
The Princess
The Empire

THE NAKED TRILOGY

One Man
One Woman
Two Together

THE SAVAGE SERIES

Savage Hunger
Savage Burn
Savage Love
Savage Ending

THE BRILLIANCE TRILOGY

A Reckless Note
A Wicked Song
A Sinful Encore

ADRIAN'S TRILOGY

When He's Dirty
When He's Bad
When He's Wild

NECKLACE TRILOGY

What If I Never?
Because I Can
When I Say Yes

LUCIFER'S TRILOGY

Lucifer's Sin
Lucifer's Touch
Lucifer's Revenge

*eBook only

ABOUT LISA RENEE JONES

New York Times and *USA Today* bestselling author Lisa Renee Jones writes dark, edgy fiction including the highly acclaimed *Inside Out* series and the crime thriller *The Poet*. Suzanne Todd (producer of Alice in Wonderland and Bad Moms) on the *Inside Out* series: *Lisa has created a beautiful, complicated, and sensual world that is filled with intrigue and suspense.*

Prior to publishing, Lisa owned a multi-state staffing agency that was recognized many times by The Austin Business Journal and also praised by the Dallas Women's Magazine. In 1998 Lisa was listed as the #7 growing women-owned business in Entrepreneur Magazine. She lives in Colorado with her husband, a cat that talks too much, and a Golden Retriever who is afraid of trash bags.

Made in United States
North Haven, CT
22 January 2022

15126624R00162